REMEMBER

me

Roxanne Tully

Cover Design: www.mayflowerstudio.com ·
Editor: Shana Grogan; The Editor's Lexicon

CONTENTS

CHAPTER 1

MATT

Matt stroked his wife's long dark hair away from her face as they stood in the bedroom of the beach house, her head leaning against his bare chest.

"How can you trust me with your body the way you just did and still be keeping things from me?" he asked, pulling her back and holding her shoulders.

Matt stared into his wife's eyes, searching and waiting for her to give him something.

Liz Owen wasn't known for having a way with words, but sometimes, if you looked closely, you could tell exactly what she was thinking.

Nothing but the cold wall behind her, she pulled away from his hold, reaching for his plaid button-down shirt. With displeasure, he helped her into it. She gave him a glance of appreciation for his tenderness and turned away to sit on the bed. She glared at the lit candle on the nightstand, with no sign of answering his question.

Frustrated, Matt walked to the window and stared at the dark, starless night beyond. After a long silent moment, he turned to face her. "What were we talking about before we...?" he kept his voice low, conscious of the others sleeping in the house.

His wife's eyes wandered down and to her left. A sign of remembering. He guessed she was replaying the recent events in her head. He had stormed off the day before, disappearing for the entire day after his wife and his brother, Ben, confessed to an intimate night they'd spent together three years ago. It was the summer before Liz and Matt were married. Their brief break up, for reasons that Matt couldn't even remember, somehow led his brother consoling his then ex-girlfriend, and they'd wound up talking and drinking all night, only to wake up naked together.

Maybe those weren't the words they'd used, but that's how Matt pictured it. Fresh chills went up his spine for the tenth time that day, followed by heat rising into his neck. In the past twenty-four hours, he'd been fighting with himself. Trying not to picture all the things that his brother had done with her. Where he touched her. If he'd been looking into her eyes while...no. He drew a fist to his mouth.

Like he said, fighting with himself.

Now, three years later, Matt had been blindsided by the truth. At no better time than at his parents' beach house in the Hamptons, in Long Island. During the heated argument out on the back porch, Ben had insisted it was his idea not to tell Matt, and Liz agreed.

Her pleas and reasons didn't matter to him. It was all bullshit if you asked him.

There's no way of knowing he would have forgiven them if the truth had come out back then. But he would have liked to be given the choice. Instead, his wife had chosen to start their marriage based on this lie.

Still, something about their confession seemed off, which brought him back here tonight. He needed to be alone with his wife. The woman for whom his love had only grown over the few years they'd been together.

"You came back in here," her voice cracked through his thoughts. "And...I told you that Ben lied. It was my decision to keep this from you." This time she met his eyes without hesitation. She took a deep, shaky breath. Even in the dimly lit room, he could see her eyes were still red.

"And I had asked you why," he continued for her. That was when he'd remembered her response to what he thought was a simple question.

Nothing. She shut down and looked away from him. He'd lost her. And it was killing him. That was when he'd decided to take a different approach. He asked her to close her eyes. She had without question. He'd turned off the lights and lit the few candles in the room, while she waited. He knew she trusted him completely and hoped this would make her feel safe.

It seemed to be working. He felt them reconnect after they had sex, right there against the faded ivory wall, between the guest bed and the only window. Until they were done and he'd started questioning her again.

"And I've already heard your reasoning on severing my relationship with my brother yesterday." He waited for her response. "I think there's more." There was a distinct edge in his voice and he'd hoped she heard it.

"You remember why we broke up that summer, Matt?"

Now it was his turn to look away. "Yes."

"You knew it was hard for me to trust you again. To trust that you wouldn't take off again with every doubt you had. And when time passed and you asked me to marry you," she paused. "Then we had that talk a week before our wedding."

Matt remembered that talk. It was on the floor of his old apartment. They sat against the couch drinking wine and fantasizing about their future. More than anything, Matt remembered proclaiming to never leave her side again.

"I told that you that we would be together forever. That you were the one and only in my life," he swallowed hard. "And that there was nothing that our love couldn't overcome."

She let a few tears fall. "I wanted to tell you right there but all I could do is picture you walking away from me," she sobbed.

"Why was I walking away?" His voice was soft.

She laughed bitterly at herself. "Oh, there were a number of scenarios," she started. "You couldn't be with someone who would come between you and your brother; being with me now would be too complicated and weird;" she took a breath. "Or that you would have been disgusted by the whole thing and...therefore, me."

He shrugged. "Do any of those sound like me?"

"No," she admitted solemnly. "But of course, as time went on, it turned into this lie and secret, and the consequences...amplified, and the likelihood of you forgiving me was...non-existent."

Matt narrowed his eyes at her. "How often did you think about this?" He was starting to realize that she had been living with this, battling herself and forcing herself to lie to him every day they'd been together. The realization made him sick. "How did you do it? How were you able to look at me every day and know that you'd either take this to your grave, or would one day have to tell me, all the while believing it to be unforgivable at this point?" He stared at her in disbelief, not knowing if he was actually expecting an answer.

He stood back as if he needed to look at her from a different angle. "How do you not stop and make a decision at some point?" Heart thudding faster as he hoped to wake from this nightmare, he ran his fingers through his hair. Fingers he kept clenching to resist punching a hole in the wall. "Was anything real? Did you need to stop and think before you spoke to me for fear it might slip out in some way? Is this how we've been living?" His eyes burned, and he squeezed them shut. He was getting angrier, losing control and he didn't like it. He hadn't come back here for this.

But somehow, knowing now that she had considered the truth and decided against it each time in the past three years, made this non-existent forgiveness spot on.

"But now you know the truth, Matt. You know and we can try—"

"Only because I overheard you and my brother out on the porch," he snapped.

No one had willingly confessed to anything here. Thursday morning he'd found them on the back porch of the beach house in what, from the opposite side of the window, seemed like a normal conversation. There was nothing alarming about his brother and his wife talking alone. They were always close. Another thought that made him flare with anger and resentment. He pushed it aside. He knew Liz always thought of Ben as a brother. Until he heard Ben's words; *You think you'll ever tell him about that night?*

Matt immediately pondered another disturbing thought. "Why now? What brought on this conversation now? Do you guys talk about it all the time, or—"

"Of course not. We haven't talked about it in years," she insisted. "He just knows how hard it's been on me keeping this from you."

"I don't believe that," he said coldly. "Nothing, nothing ever gave away that you were struggling with a secret. I'd like to think I would have picked up on it."

"You would have. And it was so hard to try and act—"

"Exactly. You were acting. When we were back together, when you were saying our wedding vows, our entire marriage was a lie."

She stood and started to cross to him, but then no doubt thought better of it. "No, Matt, no, that's not true…"

He fled to the window again. He couldn't believe the conversation had taken this turn. But it was quickly hitting him that he had no idea who he was married to.

She must have picked up on this as she approached him in tears. Holding her hands out to his chest.

"Matt," she whispered. "I am so sorry."

"I heard you perfectly yesterday." His voice was hoarse, and he was tired.

"Can you forgive me?"

He looked down at her, giving her a puzzled but calm expression. "Well that's a silly question. I thought you already knew the answer to that." Despite his sarcasm and belittling, she kept her hopeful eyes on his. He was sickened by the fact that she could have imagined after all the deception and her lack of trust in him, that he could have easily forgiven her. He may have years ago, if she had told him off the bat about her and Ben. Keyword; *may*.

But not now, not after she'd kept it from him all this time and had made the choices she'd made. Now she was going to live with it.

He gently took her wrists and pushed her back. "No," he finally breathed out. He never particularly liked that armchair behind her. But as she absently let herself sink into it, he was grateful it was there to catch her.

He swallowed hard, forcing himself to ignore the fresh tears filling her eyes so that he could say the rest. "I can't forgive you for this, Liz. You—" He looked down at her. Her hands were tight on her knees and her glassy eyes were far away. He knelt down to her and put his hands over her cold ones. "Lizzy," he called softly, as she looked up at him. His throat was tight but the words weren't hard to say. "Lizzy, I still love you."

She looked at him confused. "But you won't forgive me? So, what—what does this mean?"

"I don't know. Liz, this all just happened. I can't just tell you what's going to happen."

"I can tell you, Matt." She stood. Her voice was pleading, shaky. "You have to forgive me. It changes everything if you don't. How can we go on like this, without trust and—"

"Don't talk to me about trust, Liz," he hissed. "You've been lying to me for years because you didn't trust me." He ran his fingers through his hair again. "What changes? Because the way I see it, there's still no trust, and we'll be living with this shadow over us. The only *difference* is, that I know about it now!" His voice grew angrier with those last few words.

She stared at him as he took a breath. He needed to calm down. This wasn't their house. They would need to go home soon. Being that it was after midnight, they were stuck there until morning.

But not necessarily in the same room.

"So, you tell me what changes, Liz." His voice now a whisper. "Because we're no worse off than we were last week." He took another slow breath. "I didn't come here to fight, or get angry or break your heart." He walked halfway across the room. "I came here to talk to you about this alone. But I also didn't expect to find out the decision to lie to me was yours," he paused. "And I think the reasoning behind it went further than you trying to protect my relationship with my brother."

"It was." She was able to get out before he shot her a look to let her know that he was done listening to her. She started to cross to him, then stopped when he'd held up his hand.

"With all the guest rooms full in the house, I'll sleep in the den tonight." With one hand on the knob, he willed himself not to look back at her, fearing he wouldn't be able to walk through it. He hated leaving her like this. It felt odd and unnatural. As if he was the one betraying her.

No. He was going to ignore the agonizing pain deep within his chest for leaving her in such distress. The one that hurt far more than her lie. He would ignore it if it killed him.

He opened the door and paused, feeling her eyes burning through the back of his head. "I'm sorry," he whispered, before closing the door behind him.

As a single tear formed in his eye, he remembered his wife's words. *All I could do is picture you walking away from me.*

CHAPTER 2

LIZ

Liz turned on the light in the private bathroom and examined herself in the mirror. She knew she hadn't helped herself by staying up and crying all night, but the tears just kept coming. At one point, she'd become so delirious, she started crying about something completely different. Now, she had to go out there and face a house full of people who probably all knew by now. Her eyes briefly drifted toward the window. They were on the first level. She shook the crazy thought out of her head and turned on the knob for cold water. She tested the temperature and closed her eyes, splashing icy water on her face. In the darkness behind her eyelids, there was her husband's face again, as it appeared every time she closed them.

Liz tried to convince herself that she planned on eventually telling Matt the truth about that horrendously stupid night with Ben. She knew the likelihood of it ever coming out was small. But the more time they'd spent together, the more she had to lose. It came down to whether the lie would be a deal-breaker for him. It was a tug of-war between what hurt him more, the act or the lie. In the end, neither won.

Another set of tears threatened and she pushed them aside. She wouldn't do this again. Liz reached for the cover-up in her makeup bag and applied it under her eyes.

It was the next best thing from wearing sunglasses in the house. She put on her light blue jeans and her favorite white button blouse and reached for the soap dish, retrieving her wedding ring. She hadn't stopped to admire it since they were newlyweds. Looking at it now just made her heart ache. She braced herself with a breath as she walked out of the bedroom to face the rest of the house.

The smell of coffee filled the kitchen and the adjoining family room. Given its location, the Owens kitchen had a very beachy theme to it. Everything from the kitchen island to the cabinets on the walls, were a neutral taupe. Even the tiled backsplash had a sandy tone with a faux texture. The stools were padded light blue with a pale orange starfish pattern. There were small lanterns lined up along the counter. Not for any real use, but the kind you'd find at a beach party as decorative pieces.

The adjoining family room had a very different theme. Nothing really matched anymore. Various knit throws covered couch cushion stains. The coffee table held a variety of published entertainment; sports sections, beauty magazines, sci-fi novels, and book two of Liz's witch-hunt trilogy.

The family room led to the den with an open frame that once held two French doors. Liz's heart dropped to her stomach the minute she remembered that Matt had been sleeping there last night. She walked toward the room, heart thudding, even though she knew he'd probably gone out for his morning run.

She was right.

The room was empty. The dark blue sofa had been cleared of any evidence that someone had slept on it. She glanced around the rest of the room, picturing her beloved in there the night before. Had he been pacing back and forth? Perhaps too upset to sleep, or considered sweeping back into their bedroom for another passionate round? Her stomach rolled at the thought that she'd never have him that way again.

Liz walked back toward the kitchen. If she was going to gear up for the day, she would need a fair dose of caffeine. With her fresh cup of black coffee, Liz walked over to the glass doors that led to the back porch. Francis Owen, Matt's slim, blond, and gracious mother was watering her perfectly tended plants. If it weren't for her, this house wouldn't have had the welcoming homey feel it always had, which drew the family together every summer and holiday.

Liz stepped out onto the deck, watching her mother in law garden. The variety of plants, flowers, and slow-growing vegetables were neatly lined up along the edge of the white planked deck.

"Morning, sweetie," Francis said without looking up.

"Morning." Liz struggled to meet her cheerful tone, settling into the white cushioned bench.

Francis continued her task, crouching at one purple-flowered plant. "How'd you sleep?"

"Oh great," she lied. "Thank you so much for having us again this weekend."

Francis shot her a glance, her lip curved on one side. "You don't have to lie to me honey," she said sympathetically, standing up to look at her.

"So, you've heard I'm good at that, huh?"

Francis walked over and sat next to Liz, looking out into the ocean. "I just meant you don't have to put on a strong face for me." She tapped Liz on the knee.

Liz looked at Francis genuinely. "I'm sorry to bring all this drama to your house."

"Well, I'm sorry that my eldest son's stupidity years ago is threatening your marriage," she said as if she were simply apologizing for bad weather. Francis was known for outright saying what everyone was thinking.

Still, her candid words struck Liz. But she needed to remind her that she was forgetting an important fact. "I was there too, Fran."

Francis stared into the ocean. Her eyes far away. "Honey, I'm a strong believer in leaving the past in the past. Nothing good ever comes of bringing it back up again," her voice determined. "Trust me. There's no reason to cause any pain when it's so unnecessary."

"Why is it unnecessary?"

"Because we can't change the past. No matter when or how you would have told Matt the truth, it wouldn't have changed what happened." She looked at Liz thoughtfully. Then gave her a serious, firm look. "If you had asked me years ago what you should do, Liz, I would have advised you to take this to your grave."

Liz's eyes widened in shock.

Francis smiled, "But I'm also biased."

Now Liz was really confused. It must have shown because Francis continued.

"If your reason was because you didn't want to sever my boys' relationship, then I am grateful. If you didn't tell him because you're afraid of losing him, then I'm glad that he's found someone that loves him enough to carry that secret." Her look turned distant again. "If you lied to protect the purity of the way he sees you...then I understand."

Liz couldn't believe that this woman had been sitting beside her, understanding every reason that Liz had to keep this from Matt. The man she loved more than anyone. She fought this battle with herself for years only for it to end tragically. Regardless of her mother-in-law's kind and understanding words, the venomous pain tugged at her chest again.

Liz couldn't hold back anymore. She started sobbing. "It's all of the above."

Francis put a warm hand on Liz's back and rubbed it gently, pulling her coffee from her hands and placing it on the wicker table in front of them. "I know it is," she whispered.

Francis stood to go back inside. No doubt giving Liz time alone in her current state. Liz followed shortly after recovering. She finished her coffee then walked back into the kitchen. Megan, Ben's wife, was sitting on one of the stools, with a large mug of coffee and an open laptop. Megan was a real estate agent, one who didn't take days off. So it was no surprise that she'd be up and at it early, checking her listings. Megan hadn't looked up right away. She never did. Her business came first.

"Morning, Megan."

Her head popped up. "Hey. I'm sorry, I didn't hear anyone come in." She turned back at her work.

Ben met Megan two summers ago, when Megan was showing him some condos on the Island. They hit it off and were living in one of those condos along the beach together a year later. They tied the knot last Christmas. Liz liked Megan a lot. Envied her at times. She was honest, strong and independent. She was by no means a people pleaser. If anything, Megan's first impression might be a turnoff, but Liz appreciated every aspect of her. Her sister-in-law knew about what happened with Ben. Apparently, Ben had told her fairly soon after they started dating. Liz always appreciated that he had never been pushy about telling Matt. But by telling her that he'd been honest with Megan from the beginning, it was an unspoken suggestion.

Liz shook her head. It was too late now.

"It's ok, I just came by for a refill. Then I'm heading back to my room to pack."

Megan frowned and opened her mouth to speak when Francis came back up into the kitchen from the basement.

"What's this about packing?" she asked. "I thought you weren't leaving till Monday morning."

"Francis, I'm sorry. I just have so much to do for work," she lied.

Francis raised her eyebrow. "You teach the second grade and you're not due back until September."

"August," Liz weakly corrected.

"That's still a month and a half away," she started to argue.

"Francis, thank you so much for having us here this week." Liz meant every word, but didn't miss the hint of disappointment and regret in Francis's eyes.

Liz knew that Francis felt partially responsible for the recent events, for no other reason than insisting they all spend the Fourth of July weekend at their beach house.

"Well you all need to have something other than coffee, I'm making eggs and pancakes for everyone." Francis brushed away and started pulling at pots.

"I'll cut some fruit," Liz offered.

"Megan." Matt's greeting cut through the room.

Unlike Liz and Ben, Matt and Megan hadn't hit it off. Matt proclaimed to Liz once that he thought Megan was obnoxious and 'too into her work', and that she'd lacked warmth and sincerity. For this reason, the most Megan had ever got from Matt was a polite smile, a few cracks about Ben, and an occasional few words of advice.

Megan smirked back, barely glancing away from her laptop.

Francis got busy cracking eggs and mixing pancake batter. The woman was always quick and determined to keep her family together for as long as possible. Megan's phone buzzed and she jumped on a call.

Liz carefully stripped the leaves off the strawberries. The heartache and the distance that was so thick between her and Matt made her feel almost incapable of completing the simple task. She willed herself to keep her eyes on the fruit and suppress her every temptation to look at her husband. As she stood at the island counter, Matt brushed past her to reach for a coffee mug in the cabinet above and behind her head. She tried to ignore the way molten heat slid through her body with just a brush against her arm. It was as though they hadn't touched in years. Her senses were filled with him and there was nothing she could do but wait until it faded. She swallowed hard. He must have known. Matt always knew when he affected her.

"Morning," Matt said, leaning in, inches away from her.

"Morning," Liz replied, matching his indifferent tone.

Liz started to feel the world spinning around her. With the inability to concentrate on the task at hand, and her body in a vulnerable position, her senses seemed to heighten intensely. And it wasn't just Megan's side of the conversation she heard. Matt was shuffling and pouring coffee behind her. She glanced over at Francis, who'd already been flipping her first set of pancakes as the sizzling intensified. She was grateful for the warning of the shadow behind her before the warm breath that followed.

"How'd you sleep?" His words seemed forced.

This made her look at him. Liz didn't think she needed to speak. The burning she knew Matt would see behind her eyes should have been telling enough on how she slept. For a moment, she thought her stare might make him look away. Instead, he held her gaze. In his eyes, she saw no hint of concern...They were just...empty. Cold. Now that Liz had thought about it, it was the same look he would normally give someone like...Megan.

"Just fine. Thanks," she answered, then turned away from the icicles being shot at her. She reached for more berries, finally mastering the task.

"Oh good, you're all up." Robert Owen, Matt's father walked in through the back door, carrying a large, heavy-looking cooler.

Liz had to admit that for a sixty-two-year-old, the man was in pretty good shape. He was about two or three inches shorter than Matt. His light brown hair was thin, but at least it still had color. He was very active. He ran a general contracting business and spent three out of the four seasons on his boat, *Sydney*.

He set the cooler down by the round kitchen table.

"What is all that?" Francis asked her husband. Partially annoyed, knowing whatever it was, she wasn't going to like it.

"Well we had all this beer stored in the boat during the cold weather. But now that's it almost ninety out there, thought it might be a better idea to bring them back in." Rob answered, moving to the kitchen sink and rolling up his sleeves.

Matt moved away from Liz and walked over to the cooler. She instantly missed his presence. At least when he'd left her side before, she knew he was coming back. This time, she wasn't sure.

He opened the cooler to examine its contents. "Krane's Lager? Tommy's Lite? Hard Lemonade? Dad where do you get this stuff?"

With the faucet running, and the sudden noise that filled the room, Megan, who was still on her call, got up and walked into the den.

Robert watched her, then turned to his son. "Saw you sleeping in the den this morning."

From the corner of her eyes, Liz caught the glance Matt shot over at her, then picked up the cooler.

"Where do you want this?" he asked his father flatly.

"Downstairs fridge."

"Great," he acknowledged before descending through the basement door and down the stairs.

Rob focused on Liz. "Figured when Matt came home last night, you two'd work things out."

"Rob," Francis warned.

Ignoring his wife, Rob walked around the kitchen island counter. Liz stared at the berries, fighting the tickle in her throat. She put the knife down carefully and poured the cut-up fruit into a large bowl. Rob put an arm around Liz's shoulder pulling her slightly.

"He loves you, just give him some time." His voice was genuine. Rob and Francis had truly been like the parents she needed at times.

Megan whisked herself out of the den and back to her computer on the kitchen counter.

Francis sighed. "Megan, honey, put the computer away, sit down at the table and have some breakfast with us."

"Is Ben still out on the boat?" Megan asked, ignoring the warm invitation.

Rob let go of Liz and reached for his #1Dad mug that must have been over fifteen years old. "Yep," he said proudly. "Sydney's shinier than she's been since the day I bought her," he chuckled.

"Well call him in here, breakfast is almost ready." Francis turned to Liz. "Thank you for cutting these sweetie, now come sit down." Her tone may as well have been for a six-year-old.

Liz stared at the bowl of berries that had taken her the same amount of time to clean and cut, as it had taken Francis to whip up a batch of pancakes to feed a family of six adults. She couldn't do this all day. She needed to get out of here.

"Dad, there's no room down in the fridge," Matt complained as he reappeared into the kitchen.

"Fran, we need to get rid of all those soda cans, no one drinks that stuff," Rob barked.

"Where am I supposed to put *that stuff?*" she argued.

That was it. Liz had to get out—now. She felt the walls closing in on her. And the one person that she would turn to for support, couldn't even look at her.

It took some effort, but she managed to push herself off from where she'd been leaning on the refrigerator, her head still spinning.

She tried to remain as calm as her mind and body would allow. "Hey Fran, save me a batch for later. I'm going to head out for a while."

"We'll wait for you if you need to go for a walk," her mother-in-law offered.

"No, no." Liz's hands became uncontrollably shaky and she grabbed a water bottle off the counter to keep them steady. "I'm going sh-shopping." *Dammit.* Her voice was shaky too, now. She sped up her speech in an attempt to cover it up. "I'll be back in time to help you with dinner."

"That's almost the whole day," Francis complained. "I thought you'd at least stick around for the day since you two are leaving tonight."

Liz's eyes flicked at Matt but his expression was blank. He must have guessed that they'd be leaving that night anyway. She hadn't known what his plans were, but she wasn't sticking around and wait for him to tell her.

Liz grabbed her purse and went to stand directly in front of her husband. He swallowed hard and avoided her eyes before reaching into his pocket and handing her the car keys.

From the corner of her eye, Liz noticed Francis give Megan a look.

"I'll go with you," Megan offered, forcefully. She followed Liz down the corridor. "Tell Ben I'll call in a little while?"

CHAPTER 3

MATT

Matt glanced at the old-fashioned clock that hung over the kitchen table, for what felt like the thousandth time that afternoon. 4:10. He grabbed a beer from the fridge and strolled to the family room. He sat back in one of the armchairs. A cold beer was exactly what he needed to get his mind off Liz. Then maybe a cold shower too. Seeing her this morning, remembering the passion they shared last night...And then the awful turn of events. He wasn't sure what he expected when he walked back in there the night before. Maybe he thought she would be honest with him. Maybe there was a good reason for the lies. Although he couldn't possibly imagine what. But he wanted to give her the chance. He loved her too much to give up on her. But she was still holding back. And truthfully, he wasn't sure if it would have been enough.

Ben was still on the boat. His father had been going back and forth making lame excuses on things he needed to help with and bring from the boat. But Matt knew it was because he hadn't wanted Ben to be alone on the boat all day.

The back door swung open. "Maybe you should bring the beer cooler back, if you're spending the rest of the weekend there."

"I see you've already started," Ben replied.

Matt turned at his brother's voice. Ben was only about an inch taller than Matt. Their build was similar; broad shoulders, and muscular, but Ben's hair was a lot lighter. Mostly because he'd been a lifeguard during the summers and spent a lot of time in the sun, which had permanently lightened his hair. Matt never understood the buzz cut though, it made him look older than Matt by more than just two years. Just looking at his brother now made his insides turn. The last two days, Matt's anger had calmed and now he was leveling between a state of disgust and hurt. "Thought you were dad," Matt muttered.

"When'd you get home?"

"Last night." Matt's voice lowered even more.

"Oh, that's great," Ben said cautiously. "Uh...did you guys talk?"

How dare he? Matt glared at his brother until Ben looked away.

"Sorry, it's none of my business," he offered. "I just figured since my wife's out with yours, we could use the time to—"

Matt couldn't help but notice the way Ben had been avoiding her name. "You can sleep with her, but you won't say her name?" he spat out.

Ben looked down and nodded, as if this had been the blow he'd been waiting for.

"Don't do that," Matt responded in disgust. "Don't do that big brother, righteous thing, where you act like you want me to get angry so I would 'get it all out.'"

"I don't want you to get angry. I want you to listen to me. I get that you were too upset to listen to us back there," he said, pointing to the back porch, "but at least let me say this; Matt, she's always loved you, only you. She was unspeakably upset that night. And...you know we were always close. I've loved her like a sister since you two started dating."

"That's disturbing," Matt raised a judgmental eyebrow at his brother.

"Would you just listen!" Ben yelled. "I'm trying to explain what happened that night."

Matt stared at his brother coldly, remaining calm, unlike his quickly increasing heartrate. "I'm hearing you. You took advantage of her vulnerability."

"Who left her vulnerable?" Ben bit out, then inhaled a sharp breath. "And it's not like I forced her into it," he said slowly through gritted teeth.

Matt drew back, stunned. He not only felt a knife in his own heart, but one on Liz's behalf too. "Wow," Matt blew out a slow, heavy breath, as he watched Ben squeeze his eyes shut and shake his head. Matt had known how Ben cared about Liz and imagined how his own words would have shocked him. "No. Maybe not. But she didn't come knocking on your door, either." Matt took one last swig of his beer and placed the empty bottle in the cardboard beer box on the kitchen island.

Francis walked through the basement door carrying a bin of laundry. "Girls not back yet?" she asked.

"Not yet, Mom. I talked to Megan and hour ago. They were just finishing a late lunch."

"Well, Liz said she'd help me with dinner, and I'm about to start cooking."

Matt knew his mother better. She didn't like anyone in her kitchen when she was preparing dinner. She just liked having the family around and ready for it. She often humored Liz by letting her peel potatoes or toss the salad. And Matt had been grateful to his mother for breaking her rules.

"Matt can you call her and see how far they are," Francis asked.

"Yeah," he said flatly, silently grateful for the ask. He still wasn't ready to really talk to her but maybe it was a good idea that they were heading home that night. The hour-plus drive would be torturous, but at least they could get away from everyone, and think about what they will do next.

What he was going to do.

Forgiving her for the betrayal and the lies was not something that seemed conceivable. Could they live together with just their love, and no trust? Why should he forgive her? And why in God's name was he sitting there, struggling with himself and feeling guilty for considering ending their marriage?

Ending their marriage.

Could I do it? Why not? Liz had never once shown any hint of remorse or guilt or any implications that she'd been keeping a secret. The more he thought about it, the stronger his chest burned with rage. Working things out was not an option that he could handle at the moment.

Oh yeah. They needed to talk again. And this time, in the privacy of their own home. He was going to make it very clear that this hadn't been what he signed up for.

He picked up the phone and dialed. A few seconds later, they all turned to a vibrating sound in the room.

Still holding his phone against his ear, Matt reached for Liz's phone which was lying on the coffee table.

CHAPTER 4

LIZ

"I'm glad you came out with me," Liz admitted to Megan on their drive back home. She glanced at the clock. 4:58. She'd be back at the house in time to help Francis with dinner, as she'd promised. Her heart started racing as she realized she'd have to brave dinner with the family.

"Don't act like you didn't notice that look that Francis gave me."

"You know what I love about you Meg," Liz knew Megan hated being called Meg, so she only did it when she hoped to irritate her. "How honest you are. Here I am trying to thank you for doing something nice and you don't know when to just play along," Liz croaked out, concealing the growing panic of going back to the house. They didn't talk much while shopping, but now Liz was trying to match Megan's carefree personality. It was only natural when around someone like her.

Megan gave Liz a genuine smile with a wink. "She didn't have to twist my arm."

Liz smiled back and turned back to the road. They were a few minutes from the house. Liz's heart sank again, landing in the pit of her stomach. She dreaded going back. She'd stopped at every store at the mall, ordered a three- course meal for lunch, which she was now regretting. All to avoid going back to the house and facing Matt again. She wasn't sure if she could handle it. The cold, emotionally absent stare...there was nothing left in him...she knew it was over. She didn't even see the hurt in his eyes anymore. He must have made up his mind after he left their room last night. She took a silent, deep breath, pushing down the heaviness in her heart. She needed to make it through the night.

Megan had been considerably quiet most of the day. Normally, Megan would be too into her work no matter where she was and easily irritable at random details. But the past six hours were strange. Megan was careful and patient with whatever Liz had wanted. Megan wasn't the warmest person, nor the friendliest, but she was very understanding to human emotion. And though her sympathy wasn't always obvious, you knew she cared.

"So we're in a safe space, you can say it now," Liz pressed.

"Say what?" Megan squinted at the road.

Liz shot her a look.

"I don't know, Liz," she started. "I'm sorry but I have nothing encouraging or reassuring to say."

Liz understood that. Heck, she probably wouldn't have believed her if she had.

Megan took a deep breath. "Remember when Ben talked to you after he'd told me about that night?"

Liz blinked hard and nodded. "He said I should do the same, and soon," she admitted quietly.

"And then you came and talked to me, to make sure 'we were cool'."

Liz laughed. "Did I really say that?"

"Those aren't my words," Megan replied with a shake of her head. Then looked thoughtfully at Liz. "Can I tell you something?"

Liz glanced at her in response.

"It would have been a lot easier to talk to Matt that night instead of me," Megan reached over, awkwardly patting Liz's knee.

Liz's heart sank again. "You think?"

"I think," Megan insisted.

"You told me so that night," Liz recalled.

"Not exactly. I told you that secrets almost always come out. So if you were going to do this, then you should be prepared."

Liz let a tear fall, as she faced the road.

"Liz," she started gently, "you don't look prepared."

Liz nodded. "Thanks, that's good advice." she joked with a laugh, and more tears fell.

Megan sighed. "Oh, honey, I'm sorry. I should be more encouraging, shouldn't I?"

"So glad I brought you along! Hey, I think we just passed an old lady trying to cross the street, maybe you wanna go give her a good push?"

Megan laughed harder, shifting in her seat and facing her passenger window. "I really hope Matt does forgive you, I can't imagine having this much fun with anyone else."

Anyone else.

Liz hadn't considered the thought of Matt moving on if their marriage was over. There would eventually be someone else in his life. There was a new kind of pain she hadn't imagined. Megan must have picked up on Liz's disappointment and fear.

"Oh, I didn't mean—"

"I know. Let's just get back so I can get this evening over with."

"Oh let me call Ben and tell him we're on our way." She reached for her purse. "Oh no, the battery is dead. Hey, where's yours?"

"I realized earlier I left it back at the house." That wasn't entirely true. Liz purposely didn't grab her phone on the way out. She knew she'd be secretly waiting and hoping to get a call or message from Matt. So to save herself the disappointment, she took the option off the table. It didn't matter at this point. Now she had a new kind of fear and a whole new level of anxiety was starting. She was able to calm her earlier panic attack with her first purchase at the Center. Now she was going back to see Matt again with this new vision in her head that she couldn't shake.

Fresh tears welled up but she was determined to fight them. She couldn't go back to the house a mess and was going to use everything she had to keep them from falling. She started blinking them away, only for them to spread evenly. A mixture of bright yellow and red light reflected through the white blotches in her eyes. She quickly wiped them away.

"Oh no, Liz watch out!" Megan cried.

Liz hit the brakes, the movement seemingly slowed to a heart stopping-moment in time. Loud screeching was followed by an even more deafening crash. The impact to the left side of her head was agonizing, the pain blinding until the peacefulness of quiet and blackness finally consumed her.

CHAPTER 5

MATT

Francis had joined Matt in the family room with a basket of clean laundry. Normally she preferred to fold in the basement where the washer and dryer were but he knew she was just as anxious to hear from the girls. It wasn't like they had a reason to worry. Technically, the sun wouldn't be setting for another two hours.

"I tried Megan, but it went straight to voicemail." Ben returned from the kitchen. "Her battery must have died."

"Yeah, because they've been gone almost all day." Matt barked. Raking his fingers through his hair.

"Hold on, she may have taken her business phone too. I'll check." Ben left the room.

Matt settled into the chair again. He absently stared at the space in the kitchen where Liz had been standing that morning, by the counter. Something happened in the few minutes that they all stood there, before breakfast. "Mom, did Liz seem, a little...I don't know...shaky, earlier?"

"How do you mean?" Francis asked calmly. Matt had an idea that she knew exactly what he meant.

He held his thumb and index fingers over his eyes squeezing them shut. "She just, she seemed...like it looked like..." He took a deep breath and looked at his mother. "I think she may have been having a panic attack," Matt blurted, uneasy.

Francis froze. She looked at him squarely and gave a slight raise of her eyebrow before finally answering. "That's not possible," she said hauntingly and turned back to her laundry.

Now he was irritated. "Why not?"

"Because, Matthew, if your wife was having a panic attack in front of your eyes, I am absolutely certain that you would not have given her the keys to your car," she answered, holding an intense gaze on him.

Matt swallowed, turning away. He shook his head slightly. His mother's support had always been overwhelming.

Ben appeared out from the corridor. "I found her other phone in her duffle bag," Ben announced, disappointed.

It bothered Matt for Ben to be acting like nothing had happened. Like he hadn't done the most horrendous thing you could do to your brother and then have the nerve to stand beside him on his wedding day, handing him the bands that would forever bind him with the woman Ben knew betrayed him.

"Look, it doesn't matter, okay. I know Liz wanted to leave today so I'm going to go pack, and—" He saw his mother open her mouth in protest before holding his hand up. "And after dinner, we're going to head back."

His mother gave him that square look again. "And then what?" She asked.

Matt considered what she was asking, then glanced at Ben. "I don't think it would be right to discuss anything with you before I talk to my wife," he retorted.

His mother nodded. She picked up the basket of folded laundry and started to walk out before Matt's cell phone rang. He hadn't even looked at the caller ID before answering. The unfamiliar official female voice quickly brought him out of his irate state of mind. "I... I'm sorry, could you repeat that?"

CHAPTER 6

LIZ

She woke up with a blinding headache. Mostly on her left side. Eyes still closed, she went to touch it, but it was wrapped. *Why was her head wrapped?* She blinked her eyes open, only to realize that had been a big mistake. The overly bright room had intensified the ache by about a thousand times. She quickly shut them again.

She moaned and shifted in discomfort. She hadn't intended on it, and in fact, wished she would stop. But her erratic movement was almost involuntary. There seemed to be an endless number of thin blankets over her, and she just wanted them off. She began blinking rapidly until her eyes adjusted to the light and observing the small, bright room. A single square florescent light was flush with the ceiling above her. A worn, pink two-seater sofa rested to her right, by the enormous window framing the dark night outside.

There were several murmured voices in the room. She was able to pick them out through her own humming and shoving of fabric laying over her. One of the male murmurs she heard was clearly directed at her. As he came closer, his voice became clear. He gently placed his hands on both her legs calming their restlessness.

As her vision sharpened, she was finally able to make out the hazy images around her.

"Okay, it's okay, we'll take care of that." The middle-aged man in the pale green scrubs and matching cap said gently. He wore a white coat over it and a gold name tag was pinned near his breast. She was unable to make it out since she couldn't get herself to stop fussing over the wires and material that covered her from head to toe.

"What?" she asked, confused. And suddenly very cautious of this man.

He lifted her arm. A needle resting inside her skin under a few layers of scotch tape. She suddenly realized what he was doing and yanked her arm away.

To her relief, he instantly let go.

Another man, younger and dressed in plain clothes rushed to her side. He'd been talking to the nurse by the door. He wore blue jeans, and a light gray, long-sleeved t-shirt. He had a strong build, short dark hair, chiseled features and was much better looking than the other doctor.

"Lizzy, it's okay, Dr. Harmon is just giving you something to calm you down." He looked right into her eyes, gently taking her hand. She held his gaze for a moment. The man's eyes were filled with genuine concern. Though his warmth was somewhat comforting to her, she frowned at him. Why would this man think she should take his word for anything? She slowly pulled away and realized that her involuntary fidgeting had stopped, and her body much more relaxed than before. She spun her head to her left, where the doctor had been standing. This time he was facing away, discarding the sharp object.

"What did you do? What was that?" she shouted, feeling a lot more panicky than her soft voice made it sound. Whatever they gave her was taking effect quickly. She looked back at the second man who held her hand while the first one had injected her and glared at him. "You tricked me," she accused angrily.

"What? Lizzy, no... I—"

"Why are you calling me that?" He flinched, and she ignored the hurt in his eyes. "Nurse, please get these doctors out of here." She saw the men exchange looks and chose to ignore that too. "And get these *things* off me," she gritted, pulling at the translucent wires.

The nurse quickly ran to her bedside as the doctor in the scrubs stepped aside.

"Hun, if you don't stop, we'll need to give you something stronger. This one just went into your IV so it's a slower release," the woman warned.

Her head still pounding, she struggled to look behind her bed to confirm the IV had indeed been feeding into her arm. She observed the men once again. The first man, who she now understood to be Dr. Harmon, had been hastily scanning through a chart. The other man, sitting beside her, searched her eyes—or hoped that she would find something in his.

She avoided the strange man and focused on the nurse adjusting the adhesives on her arms. "What happened? Where am I?" she asked, unable to control the shakiness in her voice.

"My name is Bridget, I'm your RN. This is Dr. Steven Harmon. Everything is going to be ok," the nurse reassured with a smile. "Just let the doctor ask you some questions." The nurse gave the man sitting next to her a sympathetic look as she walked back to the clipboard at the end of the bed.

"Liz, can you tell us who this man is?" Dr. Harmon asked, pointing to the man sitting beside her.

She stared in confusion at the man speaking to her, the one who, she'll admit, was less intimidating. The man in pale green scrubs, who looked as though he was in his early fifties, had warm grey eyes with a professional level of concern. While the man sitting practically on top of her made her all sorts of uncomfortable. Though handsome, his expressions were rough and demanding. But his eyes... though she was afraid to turn back to them at the moment, his green eyes had incredible depth in them. "No...he's not with the hospital?"

"What's going on? Why doesn't she know who I am?" The man in question demanded.

Dr. Harmon ignored him and kept his attention on his patient. "Can you tell us who you are?" the doctor asked as if it were a prepared follow up to the first question.

She stared blankly at the doctor, desperately searching her brain for the answer. Terror struck her, sharp pain seizing her chest as the realization set in that she was unable to answer his question. Rapidly, she was becoming very agitated in her own skin and finding it nearly impossible to breathe. Her lungs were grasping for air. She was nowhere near water, so why did she feel like she was drowning?

"She's hyperventilating," the nurse reacted, rushing to her side.

"Elizabeth," she heard the doctor refer to her. "You need to try to breathe only from your nose, in order to control your breathing. Can you do that?"

"Get...away...from...me!" she warned through a deep voice as she gasped for air. Her head was turning in all directions. She pulled at the needle stuck in her inner arm, yanking it out. She screamed out in pain. The other man snapped out of his frozen, anguished look and dashed to her side, holding her arms. She kept pushing him aside, focusing on the nurse and doctor. They had quickly stepped aside, discussing something. She wasn't sure what they were planning, but knew she needed to get out of there before they got a chance to do it. Sharp pain in her head made her scream out again, throwing her head back.

"Liz, baby, it's okay, these people are going to take care of you," the stranger reassured.

She heard the doctor on the phone, this time there was no attempt in lowering his voice. He made his message very clear. "Head trauma patient in three twelve, signs of possible PTA. Need to bring her in for a CT-Scan stat."

"I have to get out of here," she managed to say, raspy and out of breath. She pulled her arm away from the man. Then felt cold hands grasp her legs. The nurse stood in front of her and gave her a look that said she had no intention of letting go. She felt something cold on her left inner arm and realized the doctor had been at her side again. He disposed of the alcohol pad and positioned a thin, sharp needle. Her eyes widened in fear as she backed away in her bed, knowing there was no way out of this nightmare.

"Wait. Stop. Hold on!" The man next to her grabbed the doctor's arm, in a fierce hold.

"Mr. Owen, this will calm her down. We can't run the necessary tests or have her pulling out her IVs. She's in shock because she doesn't remember her own name or who you are." He relaxed his tone, "We need to give her something to calm her."

"No one is giving her anything without my permission. I am her husband. And I won't allow anyone attacking her with needles and restraints." He yelled and shot a warning look at the nurse, who slowly backed away.

His proclamation left her speechless. She watched the doctor put away the needle and step beside the nurse at a distance that she felt more comfortable with. Her shoulders slowly relaxed.

She cautiously stared at the man, who was now turning to face her. He leaned in and lightly placed his hand on the side of her face. "Liz, you need to stop fighting. I don't want them restraining you." He lowered his voice to a soft whisper. "I know you don't remember me, but I'm on your side. You can trust me."

She stared into his eyes trying desperately to remember this man. But every remarkable feature about him was unfamiliar to her. How was she not able to remember those green eyes?

"I promise, I won't let anyone hurt you," he reassured, before sliding his hand off her face and standing.

She was still breathing hard but forced herself to find a slower, even pattern.

The man looked at the doctor. "Please put that away," he asked calmly, but there was a hint of warning in his tone. "She's fine now."

She watched the doctor put the syringe away and then turned back to the man that was the closest person she trusted.

"Thank you," she rasped out.

He held her gaze for a minute but said nothing. Instead, he gently put his hand along the back of her head and leaned in to kiss the top of her head.

After she'd shown regular breathing patterns again, the doctor continued. "Do you know where you are?"

Her throat was dry from all the breathing but she was able to rasp out an answer in the form of a question. "A hospital?"

"You're at Hampton University Hospital. You were brought in earlier this evening just after six o'clock. You were in a car accident that had a significant impact to your head." Her hand instantly went to the tight bands above her eyes.

"Judging from your earlier reaction, I will take it that you don't know your name?"

She shook her head as her eyes burned with tears.

"Your name is Elizabeth Owen."

"Liz," the mysterious man corrected. "She...she prefers to be called Liz."

The doctor focused back on his patient. "Does this name sound familiar to you?"

She shook her head again, as the first tear dropped.

The doctor took a deep breath. "Does this man look familiar to you?" He pointed to the man who identified himself as her husband a few moments ago.

Liz looked at the man again, although she'd already known the answer to that. "No."

She saw the man swallow hard and turn away.

He spun to face the doctor. "What's going on—why is she confused?"

"We'll speak privately in a minute, Mr. Owen."

The door swung open as two younger males rushed in with a wheelchair. One quickly went to her IV and paused, no doubt because he noticed it unattached. The attendant turned to the doctor who gave him a slight shake of the head.

"Liz, these men are going to take you in for a CT Scan. That's going to help us determine how severe your injuries are, and why you can't remember anything." Dr. Harmon explained.

Liz fought to find her voice but so much was happening around her, she couldn't grasp it all. She found herself turning to the one man in the room who had defended her when she felt attacked. He was already watching her and as if reading her mind, offered a single blink and nod of reassurance.

The doctor turned to address the two attendants. "I'm moving on to my next ER patient and probably won't be around when you bring her back," Dr. Harmon murmured, then cleared his throat "but this is Matthew Owen, the patient's husband. Please find him in the waiting room to let him know when she's back in her room."

Matthew. Her husband. A small spark went off in her stomach. How was it possible that she didn't remember him? That the handsome stranger was just that. A stranger.

"Can't I go with her?" Matthew asked, to her relief.

"Unfortunately, they won't let anyone in the room during the screening and we'll need you to fill out some release forms for her medical records," Dr. Harmon advised. He turned to the nurse. "Please page Dr. Tai for me." He turned back to Liz and Matthew. "Dr. Tai is a neurologist. He'll examine Elizabeth, look at her scans and discuss his findings and treatment with you." The doctor nodded.

"Are you not her doctor?"

"I'm the trauma doctor. I examined her injuries when she was brought in. Now that it appears she's suffering from possible PTA, Post Traumatic Amnesia, we need a neurologist."

"How long does this last? Could she just snap out of it at any moment?" His hopeful eyes flicked back at her.

"Mr. Owen, I understand you have a lot of questions but until we know how severe her head injury is, we don't want to overwhelm you with inaccurate details." Dr. Harmon looked over at Liz, thoughtfully, "Or the patient." He turned away and motioned the two young men to the door. "Please take her to Radiology."

With that last order, the attendants wheeled her out of the room and into the brightly lit hallway.

CHAPTER 7

MATT

Matt couldn't remember how long he'd watched Liz sleep before he knocked out himself. They'd brought her back from her scans and other tests around three in the morning. Two hours after they'd wheeled her out of there. By the time they'd brought her back, she was asleep again. The doctors assured him they had to give her something to help her sleep. *"The overwhelming shock can take a toll on someone in her condition and delay recovery."* They had told him.

He gazed out the window. The sun hadn't risen yet, but it was getting there. The large window had one of the better views in town. It faced the ocean in the distance, rather than the highway. He'd been in this hospital only once before. A year ago, for his father's heart attack. The room was small, the food was horrible, and his father complained the entire time. When they brought Liz in the night before, he'd insisted that she get one of the bigger rooms with a better view.

When they brought Liz in.

Everything that had been alive and beating in him had come to a complete halt when he'd received the phone call. For a moment, he had let himself believe the most terrifying unimaginable things. The visions he allowed himself when the onsite ENT's called him from a mere seven blocks away, were appalling. Even though it may have taken thirty seconds for the specialist to explain the accident and that his wife was alive but unconscious, it felt like a century. He and Ben raced out of the house but found nothing but Matt's totaled car being cleared out of the road. Broken glass scattered throughout the intersection brought back those same heart-wrenching images.

He took another look at his wife, remembering how he'd found her in the trauma unit. A few scrapes throughout her body that would heal in a week and a wrap around her head that he'd hoped weren't too far from that. He never imagined she'd wake up not knowing who he was. Or be unable to tell you her own name for that matter.

He took one last look at his wife before picking up the forms and walking out of the room.

Matt walked into the nearby waiting room and found Ben standing by the coffee machine in a daze and clearly not well rested. Matt glanced at his watch. It was only half past seven in the morning. "They let you stay the night?" he asked without looking at his brother.

"No," Ben replied. "I got here an hour ago. She's still sleeping."

"How is Megan?" Matt had broken the news to his family about Liz the night before. He kept it short and warned them about overwhelming her. They had seen her being wheeled out of the room and her confused look when they stood. He had been so wrapped up in Liz's current state, he'd neglected to ask how Megan was doing or bother checking on her. Being that she was roomed next door to Liz, he'd heard enough to know that she hadn't suffered any major injuries and that they had just been keeping her there for observation. Francis had even mentioned that the doctors were uncertain whether Megan would even need to stay the night. Had he known that Megan was alone last night, he might have stopped in to check on her and let her know he was around.

"She's okay. She was a little shaken up mentally. But physically, just a couple of scrapes and bruises. They pulled out some windshield shards off her forearm and right leg but nothing serious, thankfully." Ben focused on his coffee.

Matt gave a quick, single nod and turned back. A dark-haired Asian man approached Liz's closed door and pulled out her folder. He wore mint colored scrubs. Matt approached him and glanced at the man's ID badge that hung around his neck.

"Excuse me, Dr. Tai?"

The doctor looked up, startled.

"Hi, I'm sorry. I'm Matt Owen, Elizabeth's husband."

The man's expression lightened. "Oh yes, Mr. Owen, hello." He held out his hand. "Dr. Tai, I'm the neurologist." The man's voice was deep but friendly.

"Yes, I've been expecting you. Umm...Liz is still sleeping, can we speak out here."

"Of course," The doctor pulled out some x-rays along with detailed pages and charts. "I've been looking at Liz's scans and read her trauma report. I spoke to her briefly in radiology last night, and can give you a brief explanation of what she's experiencing."

"Please."

"It appears your wife is suffering from what we call Post Traumatic Amnesia. This specific type of memory loss can be due to either physical trauma to the head from an accident, or—and this is rare but has been known to be a cause—intense stress."

Matt's stopped breathing. "What does that mean?"

Dr. Tai shook his head. "I'm just giving you the definition. Given the fact that Elizabeth did suffer from a blow to the head, we can rule out the stress related cause.

We've ruled out alcoholism, use of drugs, or any other neurological diseases. We did of course test her for all of those things."

Matt just nodded. Suddenly unable to find his voice. "How long?" he rasped out after a moment.

"In most cases, amnesia is a temporary condition, lasting from a few hours to as long as a few months. Depending on the severity of the trauma, it's hardly ever permanent."

Matt was looking for some comfort by that last part, but he just couldn't find it. "I guess I never understood this part of amnesia but why is she able to communicate, recognize nurses and doctors or the fact that she was in a hospital?"

"Those are what we call memories of habit, procedural memory. So she can understand, or rather remember the meaning of words and how to use them," he explained. "What she doesn't remember, are facts and events, like who you are, how you met, where she went to high school, etcetera. Those are declarative memories. When those more detailed memories of her life return, older memories are usually remembered first, and then more recent ones, until almost all memory is recovered."

The doctor waited while Matt absorbed this information.

"So most likely," Dr. Tai continued, "She'll remember childhood friends before she remembers your wedding day."

"I understand," Matt acknowledged.

"As far as severity. In order for me to administer proper treatment, it would help if I knew Elizabeth's psychological state before the accident. Do you know if she was under any stress...maybe at work?"

Matt focused on the shiny white tiled floor and shook his head.

"What about at home?" The doctor pressed. The question asked as simply as if he were asking if they had any pets.

Matt popped his head back up. "Of course not, we were perfect," he lied, defensively. Although he believed everything *was* perfect between them. Until two days ago when he found out their so-called perfect marriage was based on a lie that she kept from him since before they were engaged.

Dr. Tai glanced down at his folder. "I noticed you two didn't have any children. Perhaps she was struggling with conceiving? Sometimes that can cause an intense amount of stress on a woman."

Matt had just about had it with this guy. "I'm sorry, I'd like to see my wife now. I've already been away too long."

"Of course. I'll need to speak to her when she's awake." He shut her folder, putting it back on the door. "I have to check on another patient, I'll be back shortly."

"Thank you, Doctor," he offered politely, turning the knob as Dr. Tai strode away.

To his surprise, there had been a nurse in there with her. He recognized her to be Nurse Bridgett. The same one from when Liz woke from her accident. She was in the middle of adjusting Liz's pillow, propping her up gently. Liz was awake. His heart broke to see how weak she looked. He wondered if she'd woken up with any type of memory.

"Liz?" he asked, hopeful.

The nurse turned back at him and gave him a slight shake of her head.

He nodded, with the same subtlety.

"Elizabeth, my shift is over in a few. Nurse Lauren is going to be in and she'll look after you, okay?"

Liz didn't respond. She just looked out the window. Matt only imagined that she didn't care who it was that would watch over her, they were all strangers.

The nurse gave him a sympathetic look before jotting something down in the log and walking out. The room fell silent. There wasn't much going on while the nurse had been there, but the difference was deafening. Liz kept her eyes out the window, clearly avoiding him. She glanced at him uncomfortably. He realized this was the first time they'd been alone since her accident. Come to think of it, this was the first time they'd been alone since he'd walked out on her two nights before. He remembered the look in her eyes that night. They were filled with so much emotion; love, fear, pleading. He'd even felt her heart breaking. Now there was nothing in her eyes. No memories of the love she felt for him, no fear of losing him. It was pure vacancy. It made him wonder if what the doctor had told him earlier was true. That this could be the cause of any stress she'd been under.

"I know what you're thinking," he said finally, still standing a healthy distance away from her. He had decided he wouldn't come closer until he knew she wasn't afraid. He wasn't sure what he was expecting, all he knew was that he never wanted to see her struggle to defend herself from harm the way she had the night before. A memory that would haunt him till the end of time. And brought out every protective instinct he had left.

"You're wondering if it's proper hospital etiquette to leave you in a room with a stranger," he continued after she turned to face him.

Liz eyeballed him up and down as if to concur. But still said nothing and turned back to the window.

"I'm not a stranger, Lizzy."

"Why do you call me Lizzy if I prefer Liz?" she questioned.

He smiled, taking one step toward her. "Because despite what you tell people... you love it when I call you that."

She gave him a slow weak smile. "Thank you. For stopping them. I was...lucky to have you here."

"I want you to know that you can trust me. I won't let anyone hurt you."

Then how did I get here? He imagined her wondering.

"I'm sorry for my...outburst yesterday." Her lip curved on one side. "Probably wasn't my best moment," she added, surprising him.

He took two more steps forward. She watched him with caution. "Liz, you have nothing to be sorry for. You woke up in a strange place, not knowing who you are or how you got here," he paused and took in a deep breath. "Or anyone around you," he added regretfully.

Now that he'd thought about it, he completely empathized with her reaction. People she didn't know were all less than a foot away from her; one claiming to be her husband while the others trying to inject her with something she didn't consent to. He couldn't imagine anything scarier. Not even the thoughts he had in his head about what might have happened to her, could have compared to how she felt when she woke up.

"I know who I am now," she started defiantly. "I'm Elizabeth Owen. 27 years old. A grade school teacher."

Matt fell silent. Wondering if she was starting to get her memory back in facts of her life rather than events.

"You're Matthew Owen."

Matt frowned. This wasn't his Liz talking. His eyes strayed down to her waist, just noticing that a file had been stuck to the side of her bed. "You've been reading," he said, staring at the manila folder.

"The nurse wanted to make sure I kept it, in case it turned out that I had one of those conditions where you forget who you are every 30 seconds."

Matt nodded. He'd seen a movie like that once, never imagining that was a real condition. The reality of her condition hit him more at that moment than it had before.

He wiped his forehead and took a few more steps towards her. "Liz, I am so sorry," he said after a moment.

She frowned. He imagined she was expecting some reassuring words that she was going to be okay. Confirmation that she can trust the doctors in the facility to take care of her. But she probably wasn't expecting an apology. She quickly glanced over him.

"Why? Were you driving the car?"

"No." He finally took her hand and held it, lightly stroking the scrapes. "But I um...I'm responsible." His voice turning raspy. "Liz, I know this doesn't mean anything to you, but...you're my whole world. If I'd lost you..." his voice cracked and his eyes burned.

"Matthew?"

He burst a short laugh. "Yes, Elizabeth?"

"My head hurts." She feigned a tired look.

He glanced at the top of her head. "I don't doubt that," he said softly. Although she may not have been completely honest about the headache, he was angry at himself for getting so emotional with her so quickly. He should have known better and couldn't blame her. He gently placed his hand on her head and guided her onto her pillow.

"Liz, Dr. Tai came by to talk to you earlier. I told him you were sleeping. Is it ok if I go find him for you, or would you rather wait?"

"No sense in putting it off, I guess." She turned back to the window.

With that, he let go of her and walked out the door. Closing it lightly behind him.

CHAPTER 8

LIZ

Liz really did have a headache. But not physically. Thankfully the pain subsided drastically overnight. What she was feeling now was an overwhelming attack on her brain. She tried desperately to block out all the visions of faces that were flowing in her head. The forceful trauma doctor, the overly hospitable nurses that surrounded her...She'd been hearing them whisper. Liz had not only learned that this type of trauma hadn't been common for them, but also that the nurses in the hospital must have assumed she'd lost her hearing as well.

Liz shrugged all that off. She didn't know if she would be the type of person to care what people were saying about her. She didn't know if she were any kind of person, for that matter. All she knew was her name, age, occupation, a spectacular health history, and based on opinions from more than one of the nurses, a 'hunk' of a husband.

Matt was, although intimidating at first, as tender and compassionate as...well, she didn't know exactly. She wasn't sure if she could trust him at first. He could be anyone. An imposter posing as someone who knew her, and the thought had crossed her mind when she'd first met him. But then she saw the hurt in his eyes when she admitted she didn't recognize him. It was too real. Somewhere, bone deep, she felt his disappointment. It startled her to feel anything toward him, but just as quickly, her heart almost broke with his.

An hour later she woke up after dozing off for a while. She wondered if she'd missed the doctor that Matt had said would stop in. Tired of laying in bed all morning, she got up to stretch her legs. She struggled with the strings of her hospital gown in front of her. The flimsy pale pink cloth that had four or five loose strings on either side, which made no sense at all to her.

Are they all like this?

Liz didn't bother looking up when she heard the knock on the door. She assumed it was one of the nurses again, forcing more pain medication down her throat.

"Come in," she called, finally pulling on two strings that looked like they would go together.

"Hi, Oh I'm s..sorry. Umm, I'll come back."

Liz shot her head up at a vaguely familiar voice. A voice that sounded much like Matt's but...different. She flushed and quickly wrapped the sides of the damn thing around her.

It hadn't been her husband or a nurse, or anyone else for that matter that could see her front exposed the way it was. This was a new face. Similar features to Matt, taller, with shorter hair. He wore a black t-shirt and faded jeans.

"I...I think you have the wrong room," Liz said quickly reaching for her robe and tossing it around herself.

"No. I uh...I don't Liz. I'm Matt's brother. Ben."

Liz stared at him. She wasn't sure why she was waiting for a memory of him to come but it was probably only natural that she would. "I...I'm sorry I don't—"

"Remember. I know," he finished. "I hope it's ok, it felt strange sitting out there and not coming in to check on you."

That was odd. "How long have you been sitting out there?"

"I came back early this morning, they wouldn't let me stay the night."

This was getting stranger. "Why would you need to spend the night?"

"Well they let Matt stay with you, I don't know what the difference would be with me."

I could name a few, she thought silently again.

"Okay, I might have lost my memory, but this goes beyond that." She stepped back and raised her voice. "Why would you be spending the night with me?"

She saw Ben's face turn beet red. "What? No, not with you. With Megan. She's two rooms down from yours."

"Who's Megan?" Now she was practically screaming. Who were all these people and why were they all acting so strange? And why couldn't they just say things instead of talking around them?

Ben held his hands up defensively as if to calm her. Which irritated her more. Like she was some child having a tantrum. "Megan is my wife. She was in the car accident with you," he explained cautiously. Then he gave her a look as if surprised that she didn't know.

Liz's jaw dropped. "Oh." Liz knew she was driving the car and that she'd hit a truck. Heat flushed up her neck, more with anger than embarrassment. Her breathing accelerated as she reached for something behind her to grab onto and found the credenza by the window. "Is...is she okay?"

Ben took a few steps towards her. "She's fine. Just a few scrapes and burns, a broken wrist, but she'll recover in a few weeks."

Liz was sure she looked as horrified as she felt. She was suddenly uncomfortable as this man had most likely been blaming her for the accident his wife was suffering the effects of. Her hand flew over her mouth. "Oh my gosh, I'm so sorry," she said breathlessly, as her eyes burned once again.

He stepped closer. "No, please. Don't blame yourself, it was...really no one's fault. I know I always tease you about your driving, but only because...well, I love you. You're like a sister to me, always have been." Ben eyed her thoughtfully, then began to step back.

A short beat went by before the door flew open. Her husband froze at the door. He glanced at them but said nothing. He waited by the door, his expression unreadable.

Ben turned back to Liz, disappointment in his expression. "Again, I just wanted to see how you were doing. Please don't worry about Megan. She's fine. We're all just..." He trailed off glancing over at Matt. "We're just happy you're both okay."

Ben shot Matt a look before reaching past him for the door handle and stepping out.

"Why didn't you tell me about Megan?" she asked as the door closed.

Matt stared at her, his expression still blank. This was a new one for him. His expressions were usually sympathetic or concerned, she'd never seen him look this serious. At least not for the day and a half she had known him.

He pushed off the side of the door and crossed to the middle of the room. "I'm sorry, I was a little preoccupied with my own wife to..." He stopped himself. Clearly, to rethink his words and tone.

None of which, Liz decided, she would truly believe anyway.

"I was very concerned for you," he continued calmly after a deep breath. "Liz, what's going on with you...is scaring the hell out of me and I don't want to overwhelm you with any extra information that could wait till later."

"How much later? Why do you decide who or when or what detail I learn about?" she snapped.

He raised his voice slightly and took a step toward her. "It's not up to me, Liz. I'm following doctor's orders. And that's not to overwhelm you. You should do the same. He told you not to stress over anything and try to relax, take deep breaths—"

"I'm tired of sitting around and breathing, Matt. I want to know who I am. I'm sorry this has been hard on you, but I'm not exactly having a quiet day at the beach."

"Do you even know what a quiet day at the beach feels like?" he asked, visibly perplexed.

She burst out laughing, then immediately felt like kicking herself for it. She shouldn't be laughing with this man who was keeping things from her. How would she recover this way? Liz should have been told about the other passenger. She looked up at him. He was smiling. And it was a beautiful smile.

"What?"

"It's just that we're fighting like a married couple. And I never realized, how relieving that would ever be for me."

"Oh." It was all she could think of saying.

He continued to smile at her. "Well, I just called Marcus, your brother. He lives in Richemont, which is about an hour away." His lips twitched suggesting he may have wanted to say more but didn't.

Liz frowned. She wondered why no one had mentioned her parents. She'd heard of Matt's parents and caught a glimpse of them outside the night before. But nothing about her own or why they hadn't come to see her. Maybe if someone called them, she might remember them. She decided to touch on that at a later time. She was tired and still trying to make her way to the bathroom before Ben had come in.

"I'm excited to meet him." She forced a smile. Then glanced at the bathroom door and back at Matt.

He followed her glance and pursed his lips before heading to the door. "I'll let you know as soon as he gets here."

CHAPTER 9

MATT

Matt walked out of Liz's room and planned to head into Megan's. Hell, if Ben wanted to waltz in to see Liz whenever he felt like it, then so should he with Megan. He truly wanted to see how she was doing, but selfishly needed to ask her questions about the accident. Depending on how she was feeling, he may hold off on the questions.

He spotted his brother coming out of Megan's room. Ben glanced at him and then brushed past Matt and headed towards the elevators.

"The hell's up with you?" He'd just about had it with the cold and bitter anger he was sensing from Ben, as if Matt hadn't been the one who was betrayed.

"Not now," Ben mumbled.

Matt snickered. "We're in a hospital with no place to go until the doctors say so, so now seems like a pretty decent time for me." He waited for Ben to respond before continuing. "Oh, that's right, I forgot—you have your own timing system of when to tell people things they probably have a right to know."

Ben shot his brother a look as two people in the hall chose to get up and walk away at that very moment.

Matt wasn't fazed by it. With everything going on around him now, he didn't have time for this bullshit.

Matt lowered his voice. Although it was no point now since they were practically alone. "Fine, I don't give a damn. I hope it eats you up inside." He started for the elevators.

"The only person who should feel guilty here is you," Ben called back after him.

Matt turned slowly. "What did you say?" The guy had a lot of nerve.

Ben's eyes blazed. "I heard you with mom last night."

Matt swallowed and stared at Ben.

"You knew something was off with her in the morning, and you still let her go." Ben's voice turned harsh, with a hint of disgust.

Matt cringed.

"Of course I knew something was off with her, she had a rough night, in case you'd forgotten." Matt turned and ran his fingers through his hair, frustrated. At that point, he couldn't tell who he was frustrated with.

Ben shrugged. "Makes sense...you were too angry to pay any attention," he paused, "but apparently, you saw it all, just didn't care." He stepped back and frowned, as if attempting to view him in a different light. "How do you not see something like that when it's happening right in front of you?"

Matt hated to admit it but Ben was right. Normally, Matt was able to see and feel nearly everything Liz was feeling. He'd pick up on it with the slightest way she moved, or the faintest change in her tone that no one else would notice. He prided himself on how well he knew her. But the truth is, he *didn't* notice when it counted the most. When they couldn't reach either of the women, Matt instinctively started to worry. He retraced that morning in his head and the vision replayed in slow motion. Her hand shook with every move she made. Her eyes seemed like they were looking for a place to settle or escape. Her entire body seemed to be quivering as if she was coming down with a fever. But the vision that kept coming back to him was how he would look away every time because of the exact reason that Ben had just accused him of.

"I knew she was upset, I just—"

Ben shook his head as if confused. "Upset? I think we all knew Liz was a little more than upset the other night, Matt."

Matt fumed but he couldn't risk Liz walking in on this. "Don't blame her for this. Megan will be alright."

Ben advanced on his brother. "Let's get something clear here Matt, I would *never* blame Liz for this. The only person to be held responsible for that woman possibly never remembering who she is—is you." He pointed a finger at Matt and then huffed turning his hand into a fist and dropping it, as if he were fighting the anger snapping through him. After a short second, he dropped his head and turned to walk away.

Matt's pulse was now drubbing with anger. He circled around Ben and pressed a finger into his brother's chest, seizing him in place.

"Don't you dare come at me with your fucking accusations. You don't know anything about what Liz was going through. Don't act like you do." He pushed his finger against Ben harder as the rage intensified. "Don't come near me or my Lizzy again," he warned.

Ben shrugged and raised an eyebrow. "Fine, if that's what it takes. I'm just glad that you're planning to work things out with her, once she finally...comes back."

Matt drew back. "I never said that." He glanced at Megan's room and decided it wasn't the best time. He needed to get out of there and clear his head.

Hours later Matt returned to the hospital. He had gone back to their house and grabbed a change of clothes for Liz.

He knew she'd been uncomfortable walking around in that flimsy gown. He could tell earlier that morning that she was struggling with it. He considered just going to a nearby store to grab something quick, but decided that she'd probably feel more comfortable and more like herself in her own clothes. Maybe it wouldn't help, but it definitely wouldn't hurt.

He got out of the elevator on Liz's floor. The long, glossy tiled hallway was filled with patients, nurses, technicians, one or two doctors and an endless number of oncoming things on wheels. Beds, supply carts, bassinettes, equipment. He was surprised he'd even caught a glimpse of the man with the short brown hair and unkempt facial hair.

Marcus.

Liz's brother was standing by the reception desk. Matt wasn't close enough to hear, but saw the young woman point in the direction of Liz's room. Matt glanced at his watch. The guy lived an hour away. Why would it take him nearly five hours to get here?

"Marcus," Matt called.

"Matt. Hey, I'm sorry, I tried to get here earlier, I ran into a problem with the—"

"Are you ok?"

"Yeah, I'm great. Listen, I just want to go see her. I need to see her."

"Whoa, whoa, Marc, you can't go in there like that. Okay, you need to pull yourself together. Liz needs all of us to be strong and not emotional wrecks." He stopped and lightly grabbed Marcus's shoulder to make him face him and silently ask if he was ready.

"So, what I can't tell her that I love her and I'd been worried about her?"

"Of course you can. Just take it easy." He started walking again. "Just follow my lead." He turned toward his wife's room.

Now it was Marcus who stopped him. "Matt, I don't need your help," Marcus said calmly and confidently. There was no smirk or sarcasm or anything. It was as serious as Matt had ever seen Liz's reckless and immature little brother be.

Matt nodded once. "I know you don't, I just need to tell her who you are—"

"And I definitely don't need an introduction to my sister." Hovering just over an inch above Matt, Marcus put an evenly light hand over Matt's chest. "I appreciate and understand your protectiveness over Liz," He dropped his hand and gave a single nod. "But I got this."

Matt gritted his teeth and nodded again. He held up his hand and pointed to Liz's door.

With a double knock and three Mississippi's later, Marcus opened the door and walked in. Closing it behind him.

CHAPTER 10

LIZ

"So then after like seven tries, you finally got me to get back on that bike," Marcus explained. Liz was still trying to catch her breath from all the laughing.

"That's amazing. I'm not even sure I'd remember how to ride one." She breathed out.

"Nah...it's like...well, like riding a bike."

"Did I teach you how to drive too? Or was that our dad?" Liz was starting to wonder why her parents hadn't visited and hadn't felt comfortable asking anyone, until now.

Marcus stiffened and cleared his throat. "Yeah, um, Dad uhh...Dad actually taught us both," he laughed nervously. "I don't know if Matt told you, we grew up in a small town in Connecticut, and you needed a car if you wanted to get anywhere. Buses weren't taken often, and it was definitely not cool..."

Liz was only half listening to her brother going on about their town. She was hoping and waiting for a reason why her parents haven't come to see her. Did they not know? Were they on bad terms? She wasn't sure how long she could hold out asking.

"They're not coming, Liz," Marcus said, reading her mind. His fingers were intertwined and palms rubbing nervously as he glared absently at the checkered patterned carpet.

Liz waited, showing no emotion. Mainly because she wasn't sure what to feel yet. Not until she knew why.

"About a year and a half ago, Mom and Dad were coming home from a holiday party Dad's boss was throwing at his estate. It was pretty far from their house and they left pretty late. Neither one had anything to drink so they figured it was okay to drive home instead of staying over, as many guests had since it started to snow that night. Then the snow turned to rain, the roads got pretty icy..." he trailed off and stood to cross to the window. Liz watched him and waited while he regained his composure. "Someone found the totaled vehicle and called it in. They were only a few minutes from home."

A cold shiver went through Liz's upper body. She didn't understand it, but the tears were rolling down her face as fast and uncontrollably as water flowing from a dam. The tension and throbbing in her head started growing painfully. But she wouldn't let it show. This was probably why no one told her anything. He shut her eyes and squeezed her hands to keep herself from touching the wrap around her head. The next thing she knew, Marcus was by her side with his arm around her shoulder in a very brotherly way. He didn't say anything, but looked regretful.

"I'm sorry, I don't even know why I'm upset. I didn't even know them." She leaned into his shoulder. The natural connection to him was undeniable. The young man sitting next to her was real and genuine. That was something she wished she could say for her husband. She didn't doubt Matt's love for her or that she had loved him before she lost her memory. But there was a distance and distrust that was palpable between them.

"Because no matter how much you deny it, Liz, you still feel for your family even though you don't remember us. But that's only—"

Someone entered the room. Liz and Marcus both looked up to see Matt standing at the door. He seemed to have immediately caught Liz's watery eyes and panicked.

"What's happening?" he demanded, shooting a look at her brother.

Marcus stood slowly, kissed her forehead and wiped away a tear from her cheek.

"Thank you for coming, Marcus." She smiled at him.

"It's just Marc," he winked. "Call me if you need anything."

Marcus and her husband exchanged looks, and Marc headed out. She was starting to get annoyed that people couldn't just say things in front of her, like she would shatter like a piece of glass.

When the door closed, Matt approached her cautiously.

"He told you about your parents," he guessed.

She glowered at him.

"Liz, I didn't think it was the right—"

"It's fine," she said abruptly. "As long as other people keep visiting me, I'll eventually know everything I need to about my life."

"Liz, that's not fair—"

"It's okay, Matt." She quickly wiped away the rest of her tears and crossed to him, taking the bag he held in his hands. "Thank you for bringing me clothes."

"It's only for a few days, we're checking you out on Sunday."

"Mmm-hmm." She propped the bag on the bed and started rummaging through. She picked up a white lightweight sweatshirt and black leggings, and then shimmied off her bathrobe and untangled the ties in her hospital gown.

"I'll just step out while you get dressed." Matt backed away toward the door.

Liz popped her head up. "Why?" she asked him, dropping her gown and revealing her practically nude body, wearing nothing but her underwear. She stared at him. "I've been in these for a few days, haven't I?" she asked, pointing to the last piece of undergarment she had. "Did you bring me any?" She started to pull off that last article of clothing, until Matt, suddenly instantly at her side, stopped her.

"Liz," he started. "What are you doing?"

"If you're my husband then why are you so distant? Why is there this tension between us when you look at me? Almost as is if you're afraid for me to notice something?"

And why haven't you kissed me?

Matt didn't answer, instead, he slowly let go of her arms and leaned past her, latching on to the sweatshirt by the duffle bag. He pulled it over her head and when she didn't move, he gently pulled her hair from under the hood and waited.

She forfeited and ran her arms through the damn thing.

"You're very intuitive," he said after a moment. "The truth is, I don't want to scare you. You've just been in a horrible accident, you don't know who you are or who I am. I...I don't want you to feel like I'm taking advantage of you. So, yes, I might be a little distant for that reason."

Liz watched him, hoping to tell if he was being honest. His reasons made sense, but the way he looked away from her every so often—was where the doubt laid.

There wasn't much she could do about it, if he was still lying, but she had to try.

Or end up a prisoner until she got her memory back.

CHAPTER 11

MATT

"How are you feeling?" Matt asked Megan later that night. He felt terrible that he hadn't gone to see her yet. It's true they weren't that close and though he may not be a huge fan of hers, she was still family. That and he needed to talk to her—find out what happened.

"Like I'm stuck here until some nipwads tell me 'yep your wrist is still broken, take this for pain, make sure we have your correct billing address on the way out.'"

He grinned. "Sounds about right." He looked her over, uncomfortably. "Well you look good, and a little break from work might be good for you."

"Huh. That's what Ben said."

"I'm sorry," he said after an awkward silence.

"It's not your fault," she murmured and rubbed the band around her wrist.

She must have noticed Matt tense at her words.

"It's not Liz's either," she said sternly, this time looking him in the eye.

He gave a slight nod, which he hoped she'd take as gratitude. "Can you tell me what happened?"

Megan shrugged and looked down. "It wasn't even really that dark out. We were talking. We thought about calling you guys to tell you we were on our way back." Her eyes trailed back and forth as she tried to retrace the night, then she shrugged. "We started to bullshit about my warmth towards people."

Matt wished she would just keep her story in order so he could follow but didn't want to push. It was a miracle Megan had said as much to him as she had.

"Was she upset?" He had to ask. And Megan had to know that it was on the top of everyone's list of reasons why Liz may have been distracted while driving. A stupid thing that he had allowed to happen.

Megan looked up at him. Her eyes turned cold and her willingness to help had vanished. "Of course she was upset. But she was fine when we drove in the morning. For the most part. She had no problems at the mall."

Normally Matt would laugh at a ridiculous statement like that. Or crack a joke about the cliché of women shopping when they're upset. But he was afraid of missing a single word or throwing Megan off her train of thought.

"Was she upset when you were driving back?"

Megan frowned. Then looked down at the floor. "No, actually. We were laughing."

"Laughing?" A hint of relief washed over him. He found himself longing to hear her laugh again. Heck, at this point, he would take a sneer if it came from his wife.

"Yeah," she let out a short laugh. "I can't remember exactly what was so funny, but we were laughing. And then...." she trailed off. Her eyes focused on a spot on the carpeted floor. Matt almost wanted to see what it was that had her attention. But he knew it had to be something else.

A wash of unmistakable guilt grazed her face. Matt frowned. This was a new one for Megan. He'd never seen her express much emotion, and this would top any of them. He noticed her swallow hard. Was it possible? Megan was fighting tears.

"Megan?" Matt took a small step toward her.

She quickly snapped back into the present and brushed her face, briskly. "Thanks for checking on me, Matt. I know Ben asked you to before he left."

That wasn't true. He was sure his brother didn't want Matt anywhere near Megan.

"Actually, he didn't ask."

She nodded, understandingly. "You wanted to ask me about Ben and Liz?" her voice was low.

She had the wrong idea. He truly was concerned. That and he wanted to know what happened on their way home. Maybe a significant part that the police report had left out. Anything to help him understand why his wife was in there with no memory of her life. But he couldn't tell her all this. She would just assume that he was trying to find another person to blame.

"I can only conclude from your reaction, or lack of—that you already knew?" he asked her, with a raised eyebrow.

"Yes," she answered without looking away.

"When did he tell you?"

She thought for a moment. Her eyes immediately shifted up and to her left. A visual of a real event, he identified. He had recently read countless articles online, while in the waiting room about how to tell when someone is recalling true memories...or making them up.

"It was Thanksgiving," she started, her eyes now searching. "We had started dating earlier that summer and he invited me to 'meet the family'. Liz and I got along great that night." She glanced at him. "You two had already set a date for your wedding by then. By the end of the night I told him I had a great time and his family was very warm and welcoming. Then Ben stopped me when we were walking back to his car." She half smiled to herself. "He told me he really liked me and before it went further, he wanted me to know what happened between him and Liz when you two were...separated."

He nodded. "He told you right away." Fighting his anger.

She gave him a thoughtful look, even for her. "Matt you have to understand, it was *different* for me and Ben. He and I had just started getting serious and I had absolutely no relation to anyone involved," she paused. "Matt," she waited until he looked at her to continue. "It was a lot easier for Ben to tell me than for either of them to tell you."

"Yeah. I know." He slipped his hands in his pockets. "Thanks, Megan. Oh and hey, if you remember what happened after all the laughing, let me know, I'll be next door," he said it lightheartedly with a smirk, but he wanted to know what had gotten Meg so upset moments ago. Something told him she was holding back. He was getting really tired of people keeping things from him.

* * *

On Sunday, Matt arrived at the hospital early for Liz's discharge. Since there was nothing really wrong with her other than vanished memories, the doctors had told him there's no reason for her to spend any more time in the hospital when the best medicine for her would be surroundings of familiar objects, people and places.

Home was the best place for her. Of that he was sure.

He filled out the necessary paperwork and took the remaining forms for Liz to sign. She'd convinced him the night before that she didn't need him to stay the night again and insisted that she had his phone number if she needed him.

Matt understood to an extent that forcing his presence would only push her away and overwhelm her, so he didn't put up too much of a fight. He was sure that she was either still annoyed, or embarrassed for stripping down to near nudity, needing a reaction from him.

He supposed he *could* have kissed her. But that would be too intimate for him at the moment. He couldn't kiss her just to satisfy her doubts. He wasn't willing to do that. Not even if it made her feel better in the moment. What if she could sense his anger? He was still angry, wasn't he? He had to be. Although the past few days, he'd felt nothing but fear and tension. That combination overpowered the anger. But he knew it would soon return. He shrugged off the trailing thoughts and focused on the man standing outside of Liz's room.

Marcus.

What's he doing here this early?

Everything about the way Liz's brother stood in front of that room made Matt uneasy. He looked like an angry bully waiting for school to let out so he can confront the kid that sold him out!

"Marcus!" he called.

"Hey," Marcus pushed away from the door, as Matt headed right for it, with no intention of stopping.

"She in there?"

"No," Marcus replied. "I got here just as they were wheeling her away for her final scans before letting her get out of here."

Matt sighed, pushing past his brother in law. Somehow, he knew that whatever Marcus was here to say, he didn't want his wife hearing. Marcus clearly wasn't briefed well enough on how sensitive Liz's state was and how the slightest lapse can delay recovery.

Matt ignored Marcus and headed straight for Liz's duffle bag.

"Listen, I know Liz is checking out today."

Checking out? Matt was annoyed. He knew that Liz's little brother hadn't meant any harm, but this wasn't a hotel. He wasn't about to argue. He'd rather Marcus just say what he came there to say.

"What's up?" Matt asked without looking up, placing Liz's bag on the edge of the bed.

"I think it would be best if Liz came home with me."

Matt froze for only a second, before continuing his task. "Well you have a right to your opinion," he offered casually, as if Marcus had just told him he thought they made too many Star Wars movies. Everyone in the world might disagree with you, but you still had a right to your opinion.

Marcus shifted, uncomfortably.

Figuring that response wasn't enough for him, Matt continued. "It's not up for discussion where Liz *stays*." He emphasized that last word. "She has a home. She has a husband." Clearly Matt had to spell this fact out for Marcus, since the kid had never been able to hold a relationship for more than a month. "She's coming home with me. And that's final." Matt was more than grateful that Marcus didn't know about the recent family drama.

"You're not doing what's best for her," Marcus insisted. His voice more demanding. "The doctor said himself; she'd most likely remember her earlier memories," he paused. "I'm a big part of her earlier memories, Matt. Don't you want to help her?"

Matt had to breathe, reminding himself that this was his wife's brother and probably only wanted the best for his sister. He immediately relaxed. "Look, if you were taking her back to your parents' old house, I'd agree with you," he said squarely. He wanted Marcus to understand that he did want to help Liz, and not just being possessive. "She'd be in her old room, where she'd spent most of her life. I'd drive her there myself in a heartbeat," he paused and softened his tone. "But that house is gone. And I'm sorry, but I don't see the benefit from her hanging around your bachelor pad."

"Maybe we should let her decide." Marcus held his tone steady.

Now he'd heard enough. "I don't think you understand the severity of her condition, Marc." He kept his voice firm, but respectful. "You can't force her to choose. It's too much pressure for her."

"You can't force her into your bed, Matt. You're a stranger to her."

Just as easily as Marcus had said those words to him, Matt threw the bag down and pinned Marcus against the closed bathroom door.

"What happens in the privacy of our home is our business, Marcus. Don't you ever accuse me of taking advantage of Liz." He held a sharp edge in his voice. He slowly released his wife's well-meaning brother but not before making sure Marcus had seen the fierce look in his eyes.

He'd placed the last piece of her belongings in the bag. "You're welcome in our home anytime, Marcus, but I'm not letting her out of my sight."

The door to Liz's room opened and a male technician wheeled her into the room.

For the first time since she'd been in that accident, Liz was smiling. Matt gave Marcus a warning look. *Say one word and you'll regret it.*

Matt returned her smile as he looked down at her in the chair. "You ready to get out of here?"

CHAPTER 12

LIZ

Liz nodded, picking at the hem of her shirt. The truth was she was more than ready to get out of the hospital where people fussed over her, made decisions for her and basically treated her like she couldn't walk. She had lost her memory but was still capable of helping herself out of bed.

She began to stand. Matt reached for her hand, but she grabbed the one the attendant had held out for her, instead. Again, she didn't need one, but it took more effort to avoid the help. "I'm ready." She looked at Marcus and gave a warm smile. "Are we all leaving together?"

She didn't miss the warning look that her husband was giving her brother. *Neither deaf nor blind, people.*

"No," Marcus replied. "I actually have to get to work. But I wanted to see you before you checked out today." He glanced at Matt, before stepping toward her. "Please call me if you need anything at all. I checked your phone and all my numbers and email are still there."

She frowned at that reassurance, but she was too happy to question anything and gave her brother a strong, solid hug. She wanted him to know that she felt the connection between them and whatever stir up was clearly happening between him and Matt before she came in, didn't matter to her.

"Do you ever come visit?" she asked, hopeful.

"Uhh...not–"

"As often as we'd like," Matt interjected, finishing the sentence. "Marcus lives a good hour away and weekends always get...tricky, right Marc?"

Marcus kept his focus on Liz. "I will come visit whenever you'd like me too. Never too busy for my big sister." He gave her a kiss on the cheek, nodded a thank you to the attendant and nurse and headed out.

Liz's heart dropped. She wished to hell she was leaving with him instead. Leaving with her husband was probably the right option, even if she was feeling something off about the way he looked at her from time to time.

After signing all the papers shoved at her at the front desk, Liz pushed her way from the revolving doors and stepped out into the warm, sunny driveway. A black SUV pulled up in front of her and the windows rolled down. A man dressed in khaki shorts and a white polo shirt stepped out and handed the keys to Matt, who followed behind her.

Matt seemed a bit uneasy. As if he hadn't planned for this or known what to do. What was she thinking? Of course he hadn't planned for this. His wife was in a terrible car accident that caused possibly permanent memory loss. Still, something was off with him.

He pulled the passenger door open for her. "I hope you don't mind, I thought it would be a better idea if I take you to one of our favorite spots in town before we head home."

She didn't mind at all. *Home* was the last place she wanted to go. Especially with a stranger.

"Nice car." She admired when Matt jumped into the driver seat a few short seconds later.

"Thanks. It's yours."

She frowned.

He glanced at her and grinned. "You totaled mine, remember?"

She didn't. But knew it was true. She didn't answer and looked ahead as he pulled away.

They drove in silence for a while. She had been watching the roads carefully, as if she were expecting to recognize something. Then she focused on the people on the streets. It didn't take her long to figure out what she was doing. Desperately searching for someone to be familiar to her. As if there would be someone out there that could trigger something in her. Anything. But everyone appeared to be as much a stranger as the man sitting next to her.

"Can I ask what you are thinking?"

"How close are we to our neighborhood?" she asked instantly.

"Wondering if you'd know anyone here?" When Liz didn't respond, he sighed. "I'm sorry, you hate being predictable."

"I just realized that this is by the beach. Do we live near the beach?"

"Not us. But my parents do."

"Oh."

"We're actually not anywhere near here. We do live on Long Island, but not near the water." Matt's face fell while he paused and focused on the road. "We probably should though, you love the beach," he paused. "We were staying with my parents at the time of the accident, which is why the hospital you were brought to is closer to their neighborhood."

Liz opened her mouth to ask another question when the car settled onto a bumpier road. It was loud and rough. The sound and harshness of the road made her jump and gasp as she clutched her hand across her chest.

Matt immediately pulled over to an empty space that clearly signaled NO PARKING. He glanced in the rearview mirror, put the break on and leaned over her. Concern and panic all over his face. "Are you alright?"

She flushed with embarrassment. "Oh, um...yes. I'm sorry. It was just the road. I don't know why that scared me." Matt sighed and glanced outside the windshield. "No. I'm sorry. I should have warned you about the road." He straightened after a short moment and proceeded slowly down the road, then parking again just before the intersection of a paved main street. It appeared that only the side streets were cobblestoned. Matt quickly glanced at her before jumping out and coming around the front of the vehicle to open her door.

"Thank you." She took his hand. She didn't trust herself on the uneven street. His hand felt warm and right underneath hers.

"Come on." He nodded up the road. "We're going this way." The street held an array of stores, all very different but somehow belonging in this charming town.

"Where are we?"

"Landon's Point. It's the collection of shops by the water and your favorite place to visit—when we're at my parents' beach house, at least."

They continued down the street and Liz couldn't keep her eyes from drifting to every person passing them. Hoping that a familiar face might trigger something. Dr. Tai said that sometimes seeing someone or something that came across your life once can bring on a memory. He compared it to having a full-length dream the same night you heard a quick mention of something. A few headless mannequins were dressed behind store windows. One wore a dark sequined dress, with tasseled sleeves and skirt hem. Liz scrunched her nose and sincerely hoped this wasn't her style.

"Is this something I would wear?" she asked, cringing her face.

Matt chuckled. "No," he reassured. Then took her hand and pulled her to the next window. "*This* is something you would wear."

He pointed to another mannequin wearing a button-down white blouse with gold pearl-like buttons, and a blue mini skirt with a gold zip. It was elegant with just the right amount of color.

A few minutes later Matt stopped at a small eatery, with two wide open double wooden doors. The doors allowed just enough room for a square table for two to fit in between each one.

"I'm sure you're sick of hospital food, so I thought we'd eat here. You'll love this place."

Liz wondered if Matt meant that she did love this place when they'd come here, but was being sensitive to her condition. "Okay." Was all she replied.

Matt held Liz's hand and addressed the girl at the podium. "Two please."

"Of course, right this way." The slim dark-haired hostess grabbed two menus from her station and walked them to one of the outdoor tables.

"So what do I like?" she asked after scanning a few options on the menu.

He didn't take his eyes off the menu and shrugged. "How would I know, I just met you."

Liz's eyes widened and felt her face flushed before registering the huge grin and wink that peeked from behind his menu. She relaxed and laughed. Then wondered if he was going to make any more jokes like that.

He gave a short laugh and tossed both their menus on the table and signaled the waitress. He leaned in close. The table was so small that she could smell his minty breath when he spoke. "I wasn't really looking at the menu," he whispered. "We usually get the same things here." He pulled back, winked at her again and ordered.

* * *

Hours later, after the sun had set, they drove for some time in what was a relatively quiet ride. Liz could have sworn she'd noticed a few extra turns. Which made her wonder if the day out on the town was because Matt was just as nervous taking her home as she was to go there. He slowed and pulled into a quaint development with cookie-cutter low rise buildings lined up along the reserved street. Matt occupied one of two empty parking spots with the SUV. He breathed deep and glanced at her before jumping out.

Matt told her they lived on the highest floor of the four-story complex. There were only two units on that floor, and they were both large duplexes.

The elevator doors on the fourth floor opened to an opulently lit corridor that was covered in glossy marble-like walls. The light in the hall wasn't harsh, but bright. There were two large double doors on the opposite side of the elevator and two evenly sized chandeliers hung from the tall ceiling. Liz stepped out of the elevator and paused. She waited to see if she would go on autopilot and approach the right door.

Nothing.

She felt a hand on her lower back just before he slipped beside her to guide her to the double doors on the far right.

Seconds later Matt flicked on the lights to reveal a first glance at their home. The apartment was long rather than lofty. It stretched and extended on both ends of the living room, which was furnished with contemporary furniture. An ash-gray, tufted sofa and matching chair sat against the far left of the living room, with endless amounts of white throw pillows evenly dispersed. A burnt orange throw rested on the side of the chair. There was no television. Just a coffee table, a glossy grand piano on the far right and french doors opposite the entry door.

She stepped in to see what the french doors led to and then suddenly stopped and stared at the shiny hardwood floor.

"Umm...do I take my shoes off?"

"Usually," he answered. He placed his keys in a small vintage-looking silver bowl that was placed on a blue-painted side table by the front door. A gold accented mirror was placed directly over it. Liz considered it to be an odd choice of decorating, she guessed she had once made.

He followed her to the double doors that Liz was curious about. She pulled back the sheer white curtains and peeked through, but only saw pitch blackness and her reflection.

"The balcony," he stated. "It's not big, but it's a peaceful view of the back of the development. There's a lot of trees and land back there, which is why you won't see any streetlights, but I heard that might change over the next few years."

Matt showed her the kitchen, which is where the left side of the living room extended to, following a small hallway. There was a large island and enormous cabinet space. She assumed the right side led to a den of some sort but was too tired to keep touring.

There was a short stairwell that led to the units' bedrooms and baths. They creaked slightly as they climbed.

Matt stepped in front of her and reached for the first door on the left. Liz stepped in to take in the room's décor. Silver drapes hung from under a fairly high ceiling and covering the tall double-paned windows. The walls were primarily a light tint of gray other than the darker shade that covered the wall opposite the bed. Against the wall, was a small white loveseat with a pale blue throw and ivory pillow. Finally, across from the love seat, was a king-sized bed with a large gray tufted headboard. A dark gray comforter lay folded down partially to reveal pale blue cotton sheets. Until now, Liz was dreading being in this room. But at that moment, it felt cozy and homey. She was starting to feel less out of place.

She noticed Matt had given her some time to take in the room. "This is our bedroom?" she asked, almost as if it was a statement.

"Yes, I had Gladys, that's our cleaning lady, freshen up the sheets and clean up in here so you'd be comfortable."

"Thank you. It's really lovely."

"I should hope so, you decorated." He gave a half smile.

She looked away and to the bed. Suddenly feeling very nervous.

"If you need anything, I'll just be in the next room."

Her brows snapped together. "Next room?"

He pulled himself away from the side of the door and approached her. His voice lower. "Yeah, I just want you to be comfortable. But please come get me if you need anything." He placed his hands over her shoulders.

"Thank you." Although she was grateful for his hospitality, and slightly relieved from the pressure she was feeling a few moments ago, she couldn't help but admit her disappointment.

He gave her a small smile. "Good night," he said, before dimming her light slightly and disappearing into the dark hallway.

CHAPTER 13

MATT

The smoky aroma of coffee filled the kitchen. Matt didn't care for coffee too much, but Liz couldn't get through a morning without one. With the spacious kitchen and abundant cabinet space, Liz had reserved one for different types of coffee. Smooth, hard, Columbian, French Roast, it was always there and somehow constantly running low. He poured about half a cup for himself, tossed in one cube of sugar and pulled out a spoon from the drawer. The clinking of the metallic utensil triggered an image.

Liz standing behind the counter at his parent's beach house. She stirs her coffee lightly and dazes into the cup. Her eyes red and distant. She avoids his stare.

Matt shook the image from his head as Liz walked into the kitchen.

"Hi." Her voice was flat and her features couldn't be read.

"Good morning." He managed to smile. Although he deathly missed hers. He pulled away from the counter. "Uh...I made coffee."

"Okay." She glanced at the second mug sitting by the machine.

He poured her a steamy cup and she took it.

"How did you sleep?" A question she had to guess he'd ask.

"It was very comfortable. Thank you." She glanced around uneasily. "But you know I can stay in the guest room if you'd prefer to sleep in your own bed." She shrugged. "I mean it doesn't make a difference to me."

He couldn't understand why, but her words hurt him. As if she didn't even want to try. He shook it off. "I think it would be good for you to sleep in your bedroom. You don't have to think of it as our room. At least not yet," he added.

"Thank you." She nodded once. But the look on her face suggested she was simply being polite.

She's probably wondering why you don't want to sleep with her.

The sour look on her face cut into his thoughts.

"Ugh. Coffee must be your thing," she grimaced, pouring the rest out into the sink. "Do you have any tea?"

He didn't correct her. It wasn't his mission to point out the differences between his Liz and post-accident Liz. Contrary to what the doctor had told him, he thought it'd be too soon to start guiding her to who she is and what she liked. If she preferred tea, she'd be getting tea.

He carried their breakfast to the balcony, where, although small, fit a round table and two chairs comfortably. They didn't have many plants out there since most of their view was a forest of trees, plants and grass. Instead, they filled the space with pottery and a few outdoor fixtures.

"So how did we meet?" she asked after a few small bites of her eggs. She tried to sound casual, but Matt could tell she was curious about their relationship, and how it began. And if he had to guess, why they were married.

Matt glanced at her and then put his fork down, reaching for his mug. They used to love telling the story of how they met to anyone who asked. About a week ago, it had become a story he almost wished had never happened.

Almost, he admitted.

He searched for a short and simple answer, or something that would satisfy her perfectly justified need for one. He couldn't bring himself to go into the endless details that made up who they were together and why they fell in love.

"We met in grad school," he said quickly, gazing out into the distance past the high green trees. "We lived in the same apartment complex, which was basically a dorm for rent." He turned to her with a tilt of his head and a raised eyebrow. "You and I happened to bump into each other one too many times, and...here we are."

She watched him, unaffected. He knew she was waiting for more.

He didn't know why he dulled it down for her. If he had told the entire story, she would know that seeing her in the building time and time again nearly made his heart stop. That her smile was breathtaking from the first time he saw it to way past the day of their wedding. He wouldn't have admitted to himself at the time, but the only reason he went to the dorms' bonfires was because Liz would usually be there. He had always been there for her as a friend and never pushed. Mainly because her dating life was a revolving door and he didn't want to end up being another number. One night, she knocked on his door during a rainstorm because she was locked out and asked if she could stay until her roommate, Lauren, got home. They stayed up most of the night having a few beers and talking. He still remembered it as one of the best nights of his life.

What made it more unforgettable, was days later when he saw Lauren reach for a key under their welcome rug. He mentioned it was a good idea that they do that now, and Lauren shrugged and said it was the reason they got that welcome mat when they moved in. They had always kept a spare there. He smiled to himself as he remembered the look on Liz's face when he asked her about that. The reddest cheeks he'd ever seen on anyone. He had laughed lightly and kissed her, for their first real, deep kiss. Sweet, innocent, nothing like what would have happened years to follow.

He glanced at her and shifted uncomfortably. "My brother stayed there too." His eyes burned with anger. He wasn't sure why he added that. It was all he could think of to keep the story casual and not emotional. His plan failed.

"Are you two close?"

He really wished she hadn't asked that. "No."

She watched him. "I'm sorry. Can I ask why?"

He turned to her coldly. Then caught himself and forced a grin. "Let's just say he borrowed something without asking." It made him sick labeling her as the *something*.

"Oh." She sat back. "That doesn't sound so bad. Whatever it was, must have been recent."

He stared deeper into the distance, desperately avoiding her questioning stare. The flames still burning his chest.

"I like him," she remarked after a short silent moment, nodding slightly as if in approval. She was unknowingly throwing wood into the fire he was trying desperately to put out. One silent breath at a time.

Matt stood abruptly and ran his fingers through his hair. He paced and let out a breath. "Are you okay? Do you need anything else? I'm going to head to work."

"Oh, what do you do?" He couldn't tell if her avoiding his urgency was intentional.

Of course, it isn't, Matt told himself. For Liz, it was the simplest question anyone could ask. For him, it felt strange and surreal that a woman he'd known for over six years was asking what he did for a living. "I run the Arts and Science department at the State University."

Liz's eyes widened. "Oh." Then suddenly frowned and jumped. "Oh, should I be going to work too?"

He smiled and relaxed. "No. You're safe. You're an elementary school teacher. It's the middle of July. You're not due back for a while, hopefully by then..." he trailed off.

Liz sat back down, disappointed and looked up at him. "I'll remember the basics of second grade?" she finished, with one lifted eyebrow.

"Yeah, but there'll be more to it than that." He watched her sip her tea for a short moment. "I left my office and cell number for you. Call if you need anything. You can text me anytime too." He also left numbers for the hospital, Dr. Tai and her brother. Although he debated about that last one for a while. Perhaps he'd call Marcus later and continue their chat that was cut short at the hospital.

Liz blinked in acknowledgment at the numbers but didn't say anything. She watched him without a trace of emotion on her face as he struggled internally to leave.

"I'll be back in a few hours." He gave her a tentative smile and walked back into the apartment, leaving her to her mysterious thoughts on the balcony.

He squeezed his eyes shut and gritted his teeth for letting an innocent remark get to him. The truth was he could have taken another day to stay home with her, and had intended on it. Spend all the necessary time to help her remember anything, talk to her and let her get to know him. Instead, he let himself get angry at an innocent woman and leave her to fend for herself in a strange place.

He let out an uneasy breath. But did temporarily forgetting your mistakes make you innocent?

He grabbed his keys and pulled open the door. He couldn't risk her coming back in and letting her see this dark side of him that he felt starting to resurface.

CHAPTER 14

LIZ

Liz shut the last album she could find on the bookshelf in the den. A charmingly decorated yet dark room, which she found strange for an area intended for reading and working. Two dark cherry bookshelves covered an entire wall and part of another wall. There was a dark wooden coffee table that was set between two green arm chairs. At the far end of the room was a busy desk and ivory leather chair. She walked over to the window and reached the record player beside it. She peeked in to look at the title. Not that it mattered, she wouldn't have recognized any of them. She played what was already in the record player. A free-flowing piano dueling with a muted trumpet started. Jazz.

She turned back to stare at the array of photo albums she had gone through in the past few hours. Photographic proofs which had not only triggered nothing but left her disappointed. This should have been all the evidence she needed to know that this man was who he claimed to be. But for some odd reason, it didn't satisfy her doubt. Or maybe the disappointment was that she hoped not to find any proof at all. And the reason she hadn't got her memory back was because there was nothing from her past life to trigger it.

After the way Matt had left her hours ago, she was convinced that she was being deceived. Perhaps not entirely.

But something surely didn't feel right. You didn't need to have all your memories in place to see the man practically jump out of his skin to get away from you. His rejection of her at the hospital could be understood. The door was, after all, free for any medical professional on that floor to walk in. She could even look past, be grateful in fact, for him insisting on sleeping in a different room until she felt more comfortable. But Matt abandoning her hours ago, made her feel like he was more of a caregiver rather than her husband.

Back upstairs, Liz stood by the door of their bedroom looking at the perfectly made bed. Still feeling that there was something strange about Matt's words earlier.

You don't have to think of it as our room...at least not yet.

Maybe she was overthinking it, but the last part of the offering seemed forced. As if to appease her. It could have been a natural heightened sense from having amnesia, but she paid very close attention to every word she heard, continuously searching for either a trigger or new information.

Liz needed more proof. She ran back down to the den and aggressively searched between each precisely lined up album filled with what felt like someone else's memories.

"Finding everything you need?" Matt's voice sounded from the entryway to the den.

She jumped back, pulling her hand to her chest and found him leaning against the doorstop.

"I'm sorry, I didn't mean to frighten you," he said flatly, stepping into the room.

What did he expect? She stepped back quickly as if she was caught going through someone's personal belongings.

"No, its fine. I was just flipping through some books." She turned away and faced the bookshelves, realigning the books to the way they were. For some reason, he was making her uneasy. She suddenly felt him come up behind her, but she didn't turn around. His arm circled around her to tug on the book she didn't realize she was still gripping and pushed it lightly back into place. She turned to look up at him.

"I think I know the one you're looking for," he said after a moment. "Come with me."

Back in the upstairs bedroom, Matt pulled out a small, blue glass box.

"I forgot to give these to you when we came home last night." He pulled out a silver band and a teardrop diamond engagement ring. "They gave them to me at the hospital as part of your valuable belongings."

Liz stared at the shiny items her husband held out for her.

Matt gently placed them back in the box. "I'll just keep them here for you." He pulled out an oversized glossy photo book that was stored in the top drawer of the mirrored dresser. He walked over to the loveseat and motioned for her to sit beside him.

After a few pages of stunning and carefully posed images of the two of them on their wedding day, her husband looked at her with hopeful eyes and that only frustrated her more. She shut the book abruptly and pushed it away.

Matt leaned further back onto the seat and watched her, patiently. Almost as if he had been expecting this reaction.

"I'm sorry, I...I feel like...a stranger who is keeping your wife locked up somewhere and insisting on living her life. And this is so unfair to you...to have to go through every detail with me..." She supposed she was waiting for him to object to everything she was saying. But she got nothing.

His silence was now deafening her. She was sure he was listening, but he wasn't responding. In fact, for a man filled with so much emotion and love for her, he appeared unaffected.

He pulled himself off the cushioned chair and stood. Liz looked up and watched him as he took slow undeliberate steps around the white rustic table in front of them. He seemed to think for a minute, his expression slightly conflicted. He finally approached her slowly, kneeled beside her and took her hands. His felt so warm.

"Liz. You are not a stranger to me. You are my wife."

Stating facts. Not exactly reassuring.

He glanced down at her cold hands. Rubbing them slightly. "We're going to make this right," he breathed. "I promise."

*　　*　　*

That night Liz laid in bed. Not because her head hurt, or because she was uncomfortable with her accommodations. But the unshakable feeling that something wasn't right.

While she was looking at the carefully arranged photo albums in the den earlier that day, she witnessed their time together from younger years in grad school, up to probably just less than a year ago. They looked happy together, photos of them laughing and dancing, romantic vacations, nights out with friends. They seemed like a fun pair. And desperately in love, she could tell by the way he looked at her in most of those photos. She smiled to herself, remembering some of her favorites, and then all at once, burst into uncontrollable tears. Because nowhere in the pictures, did she witness a similar persona of the man that's been caring for her since she woke up from her accident.

CHAPTER 15

MATT

Matt splashed cold water on his face for the fifth time that morning in the guest bathroom. He was almost ashamed to say he had a rough night. It took everything in him not to run into the bedroom the night before when he heard Lizzy sobbing. He had stood and paced, fighting with himself. When he finally made it to their bedroom door, it appeared as though she had finally fallen asleep. He hated letting her cry herself to sleep like that.

But what was he supposed to do? March in there, pull her into his arms and hold her until she felt safe? How was he to justify not kissing her or sleeping in the same bed? It wasn't right on so many levels to lead her on like that.

Was it?

Just before her accident, Matt thought he'd made a solid decision on where they stood in their marriage. He needed to cool off and think things through, rationally. The night after their argument, he had given moving out serious consideration. Liz might have been right. The lie. The deceptive, cruel and humiliating lie was unforgivable. Could he kiss an innocent woman and deceive her just the same? What would be the difference? No. He convinced himself he couldn't do it. Not until Liz was back from wherever she went.

Who knew how long that could be.

He needed Liz back. He needed more than anything to talk to her. He was finding out what it was like to live without her and hated every minute of it. He couldn't deny what the woman sleeping next door to him was saying the night before, about keeping his wife locked up somewhere and insisting on living her life.

Talk about hitting the nail on the head.

But it was still Lizzy. It was still her and he needed to bring her back.

He remembered Dr. Tai giving him some signs to look for. Things that help trigger memories. He wished he wrote them down. What Matt was trying not to remember were other things that the neurologist had told him. Conditions that go along with head trauma that may contribute to the "temporary disorder".

Matt peeked into the bedroom where Liz was still sound asleep. He glanced around the room that had remained practically untouched the past few days.

Normally, their bedroom was very much 'lived in'. Various pieces of women's clothing would be tossed over the loveseat and bed. Shoe boxes piled up outside their walk-in closet, for when she struggled for a specific pair. And his most favorite, endless amount of make-up artifacts scattered over the top of their shared dresser.

Now, other than the slippers and her white terry bathrobe neatly draped over her side of the bed, everything appeared as neat as the day she arrived.

Deciding it was better she stayed asleep, he quietly slipped past their bedroom and hurried down the stairs and out the front door. He slipped out his phone and dialed the number he'd stored.

"Hi, yes this is Matthew Owen. Is Dr. Tai in this morning?" he pushed the evaluator button without waiting for a response. "Until noon? Great." He didn't care about his pre-scheduled appointments. "No, that won't be necessary, but please let him know that I am on my way and will wait for him to speak with me between his patients." Matt was not taking no for an answer.

Nearly two hours later, Matt sat on one of the bright orange chairs, deciding that pacing wasn't going to help, but it only agitated him more. Matt stood immediately as the doctor he'd been waiting for emerged from a nearby exam room, scanning the open waiting area and nodded when he found Matt.

Matt cleared his throat. "Thank you for meeting with me on short notice."

"Of course. Is Liz feeling okay?"

"She's physically fine. The headaches seem to be getting better..." Matt couldn't put to words what he needed to talk to the other man about. Personally, Matt had a strong dislike toward doctors. He viewed most of them as people with a certain level of education required to prescribe medication. He stopped seeing them as professionals with the intention of helping people a long time ago. But now, he was desperate for insight. And guidance.

When he realized Matt wasn't finishing the thought, Dr. Tai nodded understandingly and glanced down. "The problem isn't physical, is it?" he narrowed his eyes.

"No."

The doctor pulled them to a corner away from the reception desk. "I remember asking if there was a traumatic event before the accident which is sometimes a factor in trauma memory loss and might affect the recovery," he paused and waited.

"What does that mean?"

"I'm not talking about Elizabeth specifically, but there are patients with head trauma—or without—who experience traumatic events and end up with some form of amnesia."

The doctor took a breath. "And although they may be actively and desperately trying to recall memories, the reality is...the brain is fighting back."

Matt frowned. "How?"

"They may not *wish* to remember," he answered thoughtfully.

Matt's mind was pulled somewhere other than where he was standing. He couldn't move.

Dr. Tai pulled out a pamphlet from his oversize coat pocket and handed it to Matt. "On the far-left panel of this pamphlet, there's a list of triggers to different types of memory loss. Unfortunately, the treatment doesn't go very far for many of them," he added. "The best one for Liz is time and patience."

Matt stared down at the list. Re-reading many of the words that stood out.

"Other than the obvious head trauma that occurred at the crash, is there anything on this list that could have been a factor in her memory loss?" Dr. Tai asked after a few moments of silence between them.

Matt was at a complete loss of how to answer the well-meaning doctor.

He couldn't blame the man for shooting off an extensive amount of information and possible elements. It was what doctors did. They recite facts and statistics. And it rarely helps when they insist, as Dr. Tai had, that they're not talking about your case, specifically. A brain that was fighting back was no doubt something the doctor was considering.

He glanced back down at the list. Now with blurred visions. Visions that instigated him, as if intentionally. Showing him nothing but what couldn't help his current state. A shocked Liz standing out on the porch next to his brother. Her heart pounding a million a minute when he'd questioned her. Pressured her. Accused her. All of which could easily now be considered a "factor".

He was certain that the patient doctor assumed he was speaking in a language that Matt hadn't understood. But his words and every word on the cursed list...now drilled a permanent hole in Matt's head. Each one finding a way to connect to Liz. The before Liz. The now Liz. How the possibility of every move he'd made or kept himself from making that fateful morning led to her suffering. He traced a shaky thumb over the colorful glossy booklet. Everything moved slow in his reality, while a live horse race was happening in his mind.

Matt swallowed. "Could we talk about *acute emotional distress* as a possible factor?" he asked with a hoarse voice.

"Certainly. Step into my office." The doctor motioned.

CHAPTER 16

For the next few days, Liz was getting irritably used to her zombie life. This couldn't have been how they lived every day. Matt would spend a few minutes with her in the mornings before going to work. They'd have breakfast together on their balcony, and then he was off. He was always up before her and halfway through whipping something up for them by the time she'd get downstairs. She wondered if he would come wake her if she decided to sleep in one day. She hadn't tried it in the past four days that she'd been home for fear of missing him entirely.

Liz was tired of waiting around to get her memories back, and sincerely hoped the life she had with Matt was better than this. She finally made her own plans.

There was a knock on the door. Liz pulled it open and beamed. "Hi."

Marcus smiled shyly and stepped in tentatively. He looked around, almost as if he'd never been there. Liz frowned and then grinned at him.

"He's not here. Don't worry." She closed the door behind him.

"Huh? Oh, Matt. Right, I was just wondering if he was home."

Liz led him to the den.

She laughed. "Come on, Marc, it doesn't take a genius to see you two don't get along." She glanced back at Marc to see him narrow his eyes and crick his neck. Whatever that meant, she didn't have time to press now.

"Anyway, look at all this stuff I found so far." She waited until Marc looked at the oversized coffee table in the den. "Maybe you can help me figure some of it out."

He rubbed the back of his neck again. "Um...Matt didn't want to help you with any of these?"

"I asked him, but he said I never really talked about much of this stuff with him." she lied. Liz wanted to hear about her past from her brother, the one person she'd felt more connected to than anyone else.

He snorted. "Just because I'm not the one with the head injury, doesn't mean I'll remember all this stuff."

She felt a pang of disappointment at his lack of interest in helping her. She picked up a small stack of photos and spread them out in her fingers like a deck of cards.

"Here are my graduation pictures. And there are so many of you and me," she said proudly, pointing at images where she was practically suffocating her brother in a hug.

Marc grabbed them slowly, without looking up. "Oh. Wow, yeah." He flipped through and then tossed them back on the table.

Liz held up a small metal frame. "These are our parents?" She knew they had to be. She was instantly drawn to the couple in the picture.

"Yes." Marcus barely glanced at the photograph Liz held up.

"They look so happy," Liz wondered, thoughtfully.

"They were," her brother confirmed, looking anywhere in the room but at the photo.

She was upsetting him. She immediately regretted bringing this up. Maybe her selfish need to remember was only making him have to relive losing their parents.

"Marc, I'm sorry. This was a bad idea. I should have guessed this would be hard on you."

"What? No. I'm fine. I just wish I could help."

"Well, maybe you can tell me what this is?" Liz pointed to the figurine in the emerald green gown. That had come to mean a lot to her. And she didn't know why.

"I think Matt gave you that."

Liz frowned. She hoped this object would have been something that held more meaning. Like an heirloom that was passed on, but it didn't look that old. "I wish I had more old stuff in the house but I couldn't find anything other than these few things." She pointed to the mess.

"Maybe there's something at your place?" she asked, hopeful.

Marcus shifted and frowned. "Umm...you know, I live in such a small space, I couldn't have kept it all..." he trailed off.

"Oh." Liz frowned and focused on the tossed photo of her parents.

Marcus watched her for a moment, then reached out and put his hands on her arms. "But there is one place we can go."

Thirty minutes later, Marcus rolled opened the metal door of an enormous storage unit. Unlike the long, well-lit hallway they'd just walked through, the heavy-duty steel room construction was dim and had only a single uncovered lightbulb. Boxes upon boxes of treasures were stacked up in the front, nearly covering the furniture Liz could tell was hiding in the back. The room truly had to be the biggest the facility owned.

Liz treaded carefully, glancing at Marcus behind her. She roamed through, pushing aside some boxes. Stopping beside a big, polished wooden chair, she ran her finger across the arm rest and rubbed off the fine, grainy dust with her thumb.

"Wow," Liz whispered.

Marcus shrugged and followed behind Liz. "Yeah, we just didn't want to let some of it go."

Liz pulled the chair to a pile of boxes and sat down.

"Here, let me." Keys dangled from his hand and he swiftly ran his hand across the seam of the first box.

As they went through the boxes, Liz found all sorts of treasures. A pair of white and gray bunny bookends, a dozen *Precious Moments* figurines, and at least two small wooden boxes of silver coins and medals. It was odd that the contents didn't seem to have any type of category. Everything seemed like it was thrown together without thought.

"What's this?" Liz pulled out a vintage hand-held radio device or mini television. She held it up to him.

Marcus rubbed the back of his neck. "Oh wow. Ha. That's an old mini travel television. You used to sneak into my room after everyone's gone to sleep and we'd stay up and watch shows under the covers." Marcus blushed and reached for his keys. Liz smiled up at him, while he distracted himself opening up another box.

"Let's see what else we've got here," he offered. "Ah, here's something you'd find interesting." He pulled out a red shoe box. The cover was creased and slightly crushed on top.

"What's that?"

"It's your sacred box," he grinned, teasingly.

"I have a what?"

He shrugged. "It's just stuff that's important to you that you kept in one place."

Liz took the box and flushed. "I'll just look at this later." She placed it on the floor.

They couldn't go through all the items in one day. By the time Marcus was rolling down the gate to their unit, Liz was relieved to leave. There was only so much she could take in one visit. But she planned on coming back when she had a clear head and go through this stuff again.

"Thanks so much for bringing me here today, Marc."

"You'll get your memories back soon, Liz. I know you will," he said quickly as if it was something that he felt had to be said, not as though he truly believed it. But then swore she saw something in the way he looked at her in that moment that almost made her think he was happy to have her the way she was.

She brushed it aside and placed her red box on the floor, then flung her arms over him.

After being frozen for a short second, Marcus returned her embrace and held her tightly for a long moment.

At the apartment, Liz moved aside the coffee table in the living room and carefully emptied the contents of the red box onto the rug. She made a fresh iced tea lemonade for herself and leaned back on the sofa before reaching for the first item.

But where was she to start? Nothing was in order.

After shuffling through, Liz found that she wasn't very organized. Letters, photographs, postcards, concert tickets and similar artifacts were muddled randomly. There was one frail purple envelope that looked as though it would tear if picked up too quickly. It was thick with a stack of folded letters. Too thick for the weight it was intended for.

Deciding to start with the far back, Liz pulled out one letter. After reading the first one, she realized they were from her mother. She slowed her pace in reading them. Most of them noted small updates made to the house and random mentions of Liz's father and brother. Then she would get to the end. Where her mother would say words of love that would make any daughter cry. She didn't read them all. Her heart and mind couldn't handle more than the few.

Liz then pulled together all the items that were about Matt. Her chest tightened, as if she were about to perform complex surgery. There were concert tickets, a few photographs, two postcards, destination maps, their wedding announcement, and other keepsakes that didn't remind her of any times. Just an insight into their time together. All seemed to make sense except for the two postcards. There was nothing specific enough in the message. He looked like he was away somewhere. She looked at the post stamp. Ireland?

Nothing better than a good old-fashioned postcard to let you know I miss you. Have you gotten my texts? emails? Can we talk soon?

Then another one behind it, cryptic.

I'm sorry. I'm coming back. You'll have to let me in.

Liz slipped those away. It was clearly before they were married. Whatever it was, she was sure it worked out.

The front door swung open and Matt froze at the door when he saw Liz on the floor.

"Hi," he said tentatively.

"Oh hi." She sat up. "I'm sorry, I'll move the table back, I just needed room."

Matt shook his head and closed the door behind him. "I'll move the table back. I'll move anything you want in here for you Liz," he smiled.

She grinned back. "Thanks. I should put this stuff away now. I'm done for today."

Matt approached her and knelt, curiously. "What is it?"

"Apparently stuff that's important to me." She rolled her eyes. "My scared box."

Matt made a face and tossed his keys to the side. He sat facing her on the rug, raising his right knee to his chest and placing a hand over it. The other hand outstretched behind him. He positioned himself comfortably, as if he were ready for her to share her findings. "I didn't know you had one of those."

"It's mostly just stationary, playbills and letters," she said quickly, tossing the items back in the box.

Matt nodded slowly. Then picked up the matchbook and grinned. "From our first date." He held it up and winked at her, as if he'd just learned something about her.

She stood, flushed, and raced to the den to store away the box. Behind her, she heard Matt moving the table back. When she returned, he was grabbing a beer from the mini fridge by the bar.

"Where'd you find it?" he asked casually.

"What?"

A grin slowly formed from the corner of his mouth. "Your sacred box."

"In the storage unit."

Matt's face went white. "The what?"

"The storage unit. Marc took me." She reached for her iced tea, ignoring the sudden tension. "By the way, do I have a key to that? I might go back."

Matt broke, shaking his head, and went to the built-in cabinet by the grand piano. He opened the lid of a small white porcelain bowl and pulled a key from it. The look on his face was unreadable.

"I think this is it." He handed it to her. "But you'll need to go during the day, I think. I don't know where the after-hours key card to the building is."

Liz nodded, surprised he knew as much as he had about the place and their hours of operation. "Thank you."

Matt placed one hand in his pocket and looked at her. "So, are you okay? It wasn't...overwhelming for you?" His voice shook.

Liz raised her head slightly, his concern becoming clear. "I'm fine." She smiled politely.

"Okay," he cleared his throat. "If you need me to go with you next time..."

"Thanks."

"Oh and Liz, take it easy. Don't try to learn your entire history in one day. It'll all come back when you're ready, trust me."

*　　*　　*

After a long emotional day, Liz laid back into her bed. She was happy with the day's progress, but at the same time, hated to admit that Matt was probably right. Taking it one day at a time was better for her. She was so consumed with sentiment and regret that she'd worked herself up emotionally, but she finally drifted into a deep sleep.

Liz drives down a dark icy road. She's driving with people who strongly resemble the couple in all the pictures. Her parent's faces are bright with permanent smiles, as if they were having their photo taken.

Headlights shine brightly in front of her. She swerves. All of a sudden, the headlights are gone and it starts to pour. She glances back at her parents who don't look worried at all. They've closed their eyes and drifted off to sleep. The passenger seat is no longer empty. Matt sits in it. His expression is hard to tell. Liz stares at him for a while. She realizes he's hurt. Shards of windshield glass splattered all over him...and on her as she spots the blood stains through her shirt. Matt seems unfazed, but her parents are still in the back, eyes closed. She looks ahead. How did she not feel the blow against the truck? Then she realizes it wasn't pouring rain earlier, it was glass shattering. Everywhere. Her parents are gone now, and Matt is unresponsive. She was alone and she was scared.

Liz's eyes flew open and they were already wet with tears. She sat up, shaken and sweaty. She quieted her sobs as best she could, but couldn't hold them.

CHAPTER 17

MATT

Matt felt a slow sinking on the edge of his bed. He shifted uncomfortably before waking up and seeing a figure sitting in the dark, waiting for him.

Lizzy.

His eyes adjusted to the minimal amount of light coming from the window, and he could see her face clearer now. His heart froze. She looked as though she'd seen a ghost. He pushed himself to a sitting position.

"Liz?"

"I'm sorry... I couldn't sleep."

It looked a heck of a lot worse than that. Her face was pale, her forehead sweaty, and overall, she looked physically ill.

"What is it? Did you remember something?"

She shook her head vigorously. "I don't know what it was..." her voice trailed off, and she shivered with chills.

"A dream?"

She looked up at him, dread all over her face. "It was terrible," she said in a low, hoarse voice, that just about broke him.

Matt wrapped his arms around her, with one hand on the back of her head and pulled her close to him. His heart shattering for this beautiful, innocent woman who undeniably felt like she had no one to turn to or keep her safe.

"I'm so sorry," he murmured on the top of her head. The apology meant more to him than she realized. She didn't lift her face from his chest, so he concentrated on calming the pattern of his own breathing to help guide her to a softer one. After a short moment, she caught on and her breathing returned to a normal pace. He sat up slightly to draw her in and pull the covers over them. She nestled into him, her white silk slip-on slightly damp. He slid his fingers around the back of her neck, lifting her hair that clung to her clammy skin. He leaned in and blew softly behind her neck, stroking her hair away.

God only knew what her nightmare could have been about. What it meant to her and how much of it was true.

He watched his wife in a peaceful slumber for a few minutes when waking up that morning. He missed her presence next to him in the mornings. The way her head comfortably sank into the pillow. Nothing mattered at that moment. Not the lies, not the betrayal that tore through his heart. All that mattered was how safe she felt spending the night in his arms. He remembered the last time he'd held her, the night before her accident — his pathetic attempt to make her trust and open up to him. Guilt washed through him, starting from his cheekbones and stopping somewhere in his heart. He shifted away from her, feeling unworthy of the innocent woman he held.

He clenched his teeth. He moved too quickly.

She groaned and opened her eyes, blinking rapidly. She focused on him and smiled, that bright smile that reached her eyes.

"Good Morning," he smiled back.

"Are you okay?" her voice raspy. He missed that morning voice of hers.

"Only if you are."

She stretched and glanced around. "Are you sure this isn't our bedroom? I felt so much more relaxed here," she breathed tranquilly.

Matt leaned in to her. "Because you were with me," he whispered. "Where you belong."

Liz only responded with about a million goosebumps lining up on her exposed arm. Matt glanced down and rubbed her long, toned arm gently. He kissed her forehead lightly then backed away to look at her.

"You feel like talking about your dream?"

Liz stared at Matt as if she couldn't decide if she could trust him. "No," she shook her head, then added, "It's a little hazy anyway."

Matt nodded but wished she would tell him what spooked her. "Okay," he gave her a small smile, then stood. "I'll let you get dressed while I make us some breakfast," he added while slipping on his jeans and t-shirt.

Matt descended the stairs while Liz took a long shower. It was slightly later in the morning than when they normally had their breakfast. Matt was grateful for the extra sleep Liz got that night. He wondered if her nightmare was a memory she might not realize. A horrid thought crossed his mind with the realization that her first memory might be of their fight the night before her accident. Or the night she'd spent with his brother...might cause some confusion.

He shook the thought out of his mind and checked his phone. He already had a few missed calls from his mother until she finally texted.

Text 1: *Call me. Your dad needs you today.*

Text 2: *I can't watch him attack that thing alone, Matt. And Ben's not answering.*

Matt shook his head and threw his phone down. He was starting to regret telling his parents his summer schedule.

"Something wrong?" Liz finally joined him on the balcony. She wore an ivory sundress with a navy belt.

"I think my dad is trying to save Sydney, even though we all think he should donate her."

Liz frowned.

Matt sighed. "Sorry. Sydney is my dad's boat. It doesn't really work well anymore. And if it does, you can't take it too far." He handed Liz her tea. "Short of getting a new engine, Sydney's pretty much dead."

"That's so sad," Liz said, sitting in her usual chair. Only this time, an orange throw pillow was placed on it. Matt liked that she was finding little ways to make herself comfortable.

Matt shook his head. "He's always spent way too much time on that thing, anyway." He looked at her. "I'm sorry, I'm going to have to go over there to help him."

She nodded and stared into her tea.

"Liz, I really wanted to spend the day with you." He meant it. He wanted nothing more than to keep holding her the rest of the day and reassure her that she was safe with him.

She set down her tea and stood, smiling politely. "I'll be here when you get back."

He took a few short steps toward her and grinned. He lifted her face to kiss her forehead. This time she stood on her tip toes, tilted her head back and caught his lips with hers.

After the initial shock, he eased into her familiar kiss, the warmth of her lips spreading through his body. With his fingers around her neck and his thumbs resting under her ears, he finally dropped whatever guard he was holding against her and kissed her back. A blend of passion and relief washing through him, because he needed this. He didn't realize how much he had needed to kiss her. Even now her lips could easily relieve the pressure and burden building inside him for the past week. He wanted to melt into her. But that was her job. Much like their first kiss, which he'd never forget. He deepened the kiss, taking a step closer to her as she moved back. He could feel her heart racing. Matt urged himself to pull away before the only place he would end up going was upstairs. He opened his eyes and gave a slow smile with his lips still on hers. She pulled away slowly, her cheeks beaming a bright red and her eyes blinking. Perhaps she hadn't realized what she was in for when she offered him an innocent kiss.

He smiled to himself. "I won't be long," he reassured before grabbing his keys and bolting, his heart still racing. His brain insisting he get out of there as fast as he could.

An hour later, Matt pushed past his parent's back door. "What the hell, Dad. Don't you know I have a w—"

His mother came rushing out of the kitchen.

"Shh...he doesn't know I called you."

"What?" She had to be kidding.

"I think Sydney's finally called it a day yesterday and your dad's refusing to pull the plug. You've got to talk to him, sweetheart."

Matt ran his fingers through his hair, frustrated with his new impossible assignment.

"How's Liz?" she asked after giving him a moment.

Matt glanced out the window at his dad on the boat. He shook his head. "I don't know, mom, I haven't seen her," he answered, agitated. Letting her know Liz is still not herself.

"Matthew," she hissed.

"What do you want me to say? I feel like I'm living with a woman I kidnapped from the hospital who looks exactly like my wife. Only she keeps looking at me like..." He couldn't bring himself to say the words. The look that haunted him. As if she were asking him, how long are you going to keep me a prisoner here, and when can I go home.

That was up until this morning. When she seemed to have happily woken up in his arms.

Matt shuddered. "I'm going to go help dad."

"Matt," his mother's warning voice called as he held his hand on the doorknob. "I didn't ask you to come here today," she raised an eyebrow at him.

Matt grinned widely. "No, mom," he paused and opened the door. "It was more like threatened," he muttered loudly.

He spotted his old man on the top deck, pulling on the latch to unhook the ropes.

"Dad," Matt called, hastily.

Rob looked up at his son. Then dropped his head and shook it. "Your mother call you?"

"What are you doing out here?"

"Workin' on the boat."

"Don't give me that crap. Dad, Sydney's been gone for the last two years, you can't keep shining her and trying to bring her back to life. You need to let it go."

His dad barely paused at his task. "I don't give up that easily, son," his father announced bitterly.

Matt watched his father for a minute. Considering if his words were deliberate. "What is it this time?" Matt asked flatly, staring hard at his father.

"The alternator isn't charging." Rob pointed with his screwdriver.

"Can't you get a new one?"

"It's a four-hundred-dollar part!" Rob complained.

"Well, it's not going to burst back into life because you fiddled with it, dad. You'll need to completely rebuild it or get a new one." Matt was starting to lose his patience.

"How's Liz?" Rob asked almost immediately.

"She's fine." Matt shook his head. He couldn't believe he'd left her today to help with something so pointless. "And why does mom think she has no right to tell you to get rid of this thing?" he snapped.

"Is that what she said?"

Matt pressed his lips and then muttered a curse. "Not in so many words."

Rob held up the screwdriver and stalled as if he were looking for the right place to aim it. Then he chucked the thing back into the tool box. He looked up at his son and gave him a single nod and slap on the back. "Let's go inside."

When Matt and his father got back to the kitchen, Ben was there with Francis. His brother held just about the same look Matt had when he walked in.

"Dad, what's going on? You messin' up my clean work already?"

"Alternator went," Rob said bitterly.

"That's like a four-hundred-dollar part!" Ben shouted.

Francis shot her husband an angry look and threw her hands in the air.

"I know, I know." Rob held his hands up in defense. "Look, maybe I can fix it."

"What's the point, just buy the new part, like we all know you'll end up doing." Francis threw her dish rag on the counter and stormed out the back door.

Rob shot Matt and Ben an exhausted look and followed behind, leaving the two brothers alone in the kitchen.

The silence in the room intensified with every second that passed by.

"We could stand here till winter or we could talk," Ben offered.

"Is there a third option?" Matt muttered.

"No."

"I didn't come here to talk to you." He pulled his keys off the kitchen counter and headed for the back door. "Tell them I had to get back."

Ben sighed. "Matt, you can't keep blowing me off. Not until you at least give me a chance to explain. You've already given as much to Liz."

Matt *had* given Liz a chance to explain. A chance to somehow make him understand the reasoning behind the lie. "I did. And it didn't end well for her."

Ben rubbed his temples. "Look, I'm sorry about what happened. It was a weird situation and we weren't thinking—"

"Do I need to hear all this again?"

Ben stared at him and continued. "You'd left her. I was angry at you for making such a stupid choice, and she was hurt. We had a few to drink and let our emotions get the best of us." He took a few steps toward Matt. "It was a mistake and we were out of our minds with guilt."

"Guilt? Oh well that makes it all better then," he glared back.

"It wasn't easy," he barked. "You returned from whatever escape you needed from reality, so ready to get back with her..."

"I'm not getting into that with you. It's none of your business." Matt wiggled his keys but was unable to move.

"You ever wonder about how easy it was for her to forgive you when you came back?" Ben continued.

He had. He had considered himself to be the luckiest man alive after he'd returned from Ireland and begged Liz to take him back, promising her to be the man she fell in love with, a man she could trust, someone who would never again let her down.

And she had, without a blink of an eye.

He had fled to Ireland for the summer in one of those volunteer teachers' summer abroad programs after grad school. He couldn't explain his decision in any kind of words that would make Liz understand. The truth had been that he needed to explore and see the world.

And he wanted to do it by himself.

He never could truly forget the shattered look in her eyes when he told her not to wait for him.

It was that same look he was sure that Ben saw and consoled. Matt shuttered silently at the thought.

"I did," Matt replied quietly.

"It wasn't just the guilt, Matt, she loved and missed you terribly. All she wanted to do is forget the mistake she made with me and move on."

Matt's face burned with rage when he wondered how much of the topic Liz had shared with Ben. "Is that what she told you?"

"I wanted her to tell you. I didn't want to keep this from you, Matt."

Matt rubbed his forehead, unable to keep from asking this next thing. "But *she* did, right?" he asked quietly.

For the first time since Matt walked in to that kitchen, Ben had nothing to say.

Matt shrugged. "Can't say I blame her. I mean if you think about it, what did you have to lose? Your brother's girlfriend would tell him the truth—there's no way he could marry her knowing this. Down the tubes goes that relationship, and eventually he'd meet someone new and move on, and you wouldn't have to keep looking at the woman who you betrayed your brother with." Matt glared at Ben again. "Sound about right?"

Ben held a tight glare. "That's nowhere near right."

Matt started to feel sick thinking about it. "Tell mom and dad I had to go."

CHAPTER 18

LIZ

Time seemed to flow like raw honey dripping off a spoon as Liz lay there, staring at the ceiling. She turned her head to the spot where a mere two hours ago, Matt had managed to completely dissolve her scrutiny with that deep desirous kiss. She hadn't planned on hooking him into a kiss on the lips, it was innocently impulsive. Frankly, she was getting tired of his meaningless appeasing kisses on her forehead. Like she was some child.

That was going to stop.

Just as she felt herself slipping under the warm dark blanket of sleep, she jumped at the knock on the door.

It wouldn't have been Matt, she knew he'd be gone most of the day on his dad's boat. She forced herself not to wonder why he wouldn't ask her to come along. For reasons she had yet to understand, he probably assumed it was for the best.

With her eyes sweeping the room for tidiness, she stood and headed to the door, pulling it open without a thought.

She found herself staring at a woman who looked vaguely familiar. Her dark curls settling just over her shoulders, she was slightly darker skinned than Liz and had big gray eyes. She reminded her of Matt's brother Ben. She suddenly remembered why.

"Megan, right?"

The woman's eyes widened in a mixture of surprise and hope.

"Yes," she exclaimed. "You—."

Liz drew a polite smile. "I remember you from the hospital. I think I saw you through my window with Ben."

Megan inhaled a slow breath. "Oh."

"Come in."

She pulled off one strap from her shoulder bag and withdrew a paper bag. "I know Matt's not home, so I thought I'd stop by to keep you company."

Liz's heart caught in her throat at the small cast covering Megan's wrist and part of her hand. She must have stared a second too long because Megan glanced down at it.

"It's not your fault, Liz. Please know that." She held up the brown paper bag. "I brought cannoli's," she offered, happily. "You're going to love them."

"I'm so glad your here." Liz closed the door and motioned for Megan to come in further. "I haven't had a woman to talk to since I woke up—except for the nurses. I'll make us some tea."

"Tea?" Megan grimaced, then shook her head. "You've really lost your mind. Okay, grab your keys—I'm taking you out."

Liz stood there for a long second, as if she didn't know if she should oblige.

Megan rolled her eyes and reached in the bowl by the front door. Dangling the metal in her fingers, she pulled open the door and held it for Liz. "After you."

Thirty short minutes later, they were seated in the outdoor section of a quaint corner cafe in town with high, soaring blue umbrellas. The small table area that only fit about four two-seater tables, was fenced in and faced a quiet intersection. Jazz music, similar to what Liz had been listening to back in the den, was pouring out of the open double doors. Megan had ordered them mimosas and pulled out the brown paper bag of sweets.

"So, how's life been?" She leaned back and raised an eyebrow at her sister in law.

Liz formed a slow smile. She was surprised and relieved at how abrupt and familiar Megan spoke to her. Though it was truly refreshing, Liz was ineluctably cynical about the people surrounding her, claiming to know her. She couldn't help it. The only person she had trusted instantly was her brother Marcus.

"Lucky to be alive from what I hear," Liz responded.

Megan inhaled deeply, as if she had been bracing for this conversation. "I'm sorry I didn't stop by to see you at the hospital. I just..." she swallowed, quickly. "I didn't want to mess with your recovery."

Liz could tell Megan was not a soft person, or one to show much emotion. But she didn't think that was an excuse not to visit her when she was just next door. Liz then wondered if this was something she should blow off or confront. What would pre-amnesia Liz do? She guessed it didn't matter. *This* Liz needed everything explained. Something told her Megan would appreciate the candidness.

Liz took a sip of her fizzy drink. "I can imagine it's not easy seeing someone who got the worse end of the stick."

By the shocked look on Megan's face, Liz's question was answered. She wasn't the type of person to confront.

"You're right. There was no reason I shouldn't have come to see you."

"What happened?"

Megan leaned back, glancing at her glass. "Every body's favorite question."

Liz raised an eyebrow.

Megan's eyes were lost in the flute she spun between her fingers. She took a breath and hesitated. Then looked at Liz. "You're not at fault, Liz."

"How's that possible? Why do people keep saying that? I was the one driving." And from what she remembered from the report she snuck a few glances at, the other driver in the truck insisted she ran the light. It had to have been her fault.

"Am I that bad of a driver or was I just distracted?" Liz hated to push the only female friend she had, but she needed to understand why she was sitting there with no memory of who she is.

Megan, who had been watching her with what could pass for concern, finally sat up in her chair. "Liz, it wasn't you. It was me. I distracted you with something."

Liz stared at Megan, waiting. There was regret in her voice. "What?" Liz finally asked.

"It...well it was about Matt."

Liz wasn't expecting that. "Matt?"

Megan glanced around. "Before I get into detail...how has life been with Matt since you came home?"

Liz was sure she was about to get confirmation that there had have been problems before. Her faithful sister in law was hinting at something. Liz cleared her throat and glanced to look anywhere but at the woman asking her this private question. "Distant."

Megan nodded and narrowed her eyes at Liz. "Has he kissed you?"

"Not as much as I'd imagined," Liz admitted. Liz kept her eyes on the stem of her glass, then glanced up at Megan, who's expression was very unreadable. "But he doesn't want to overwhelm me," Liz continued.

"None of us want to do anything to make your condition worse or scare you," she paused, as if there were an afterthought there. But then just as quickly, Megan had changed her mind. "Tell me more."

"There isn't much else. Matt doesn't have much to say about our life. He didn't even want to tell me how we met." Liz paused, she felt guilty for not giving her husband credit where it counted. "But he cares. He worries about me. And he makes delicious meals."

Megan took a bite of her cannoli. "Sounds like my grandmothers' caretaker."

Liz's instant stare at Megan must have told her that she'd just hit the nail on the head. "Is there something he isn't telling me?"

Megan's eyes dilated and she looked down at Liz's plate. "You're letting a good pastry go to waste."

Liz didn't take her eyes off Megan's. "Are we leaving?"

"Liz, you need to go home and make your husband stop ignoring you. Challenge him. Make him remember that you are still his wife. Maybe that's what you need to help you remember."

*   *   *

Matt didn't want to talk much after he'd come home. His complete transformation from earlier that same day was disappointing. She wondered what happened at his parents' house.

Liz was growing tired of being pushed aside like some estranged family member asking too many questions. Short of glancing at her every once in a while, Matt barely acknowledged Liz that evening.

After Matt came into her bedroom that night to shower in the master bath, Liz decided to test the waters with her so-called husband and slipped on a black silk nighty and freshened up. She dimmed the lights, turned down the bed and waited, anxiously. When the shower shut off, her heart raced. She didn't have time to panic or back out of her deliberations. She was going through with this. As the door opened, she swallowed and suddenly found it difficult to breathe.

Matt stepped out of the bathroom with his hair raked back and a dark blue towel around his waist. He glanced around the darkened room and then focused on her. His tanned, bare torso glistened in the dim light.

The room was so quiet, she could have sworn he could also hear the loud thumping of her heart.

"What's going on?" he asked.

"I wanted to ask you the same thing," she replied, casually. "You haven't said much since you got home today." She took two deliberate steps towards him.

Matt's eyes drifted to the bare floor he stood on. Avoiding hers. "Liz—"

She ignored the evading gesture and reached out to touch his chiseled chest. His body still damp but smooth. Still looking away, he inhaled what sounded like an angry breath, which made her freeze in place. She only gave him a few seconds to do or say something, but when he didn't, she continued gliding her fingers up to his shoulders and then down his arm. He squeezed his eyes shut and swallowed. Fighting a mystery emotion.

When he finally looked up at her, there was a beat where it seemed as if he was about to give in to her and crush her lips with his.

But instead, he wrapped his fingers around her wrist and gently lowered it to her side.

"Why are you avoiding me?" she whispered.

"I'm not avoiding you." He walked around her to the dresser. "I'm just giving you—."

"I don't want space," she snapped, annoyed at his pathetic blow off. "I just need to know why..." she watched him and then finally huffed and spun in the other direction. "Forget it."

Two short beats later, her left arm was being pulled and her waist grabbed from the opposite side. He spun her to face him before she could catch her breath. Their noses barely touching.

He spoke in a low murmur. "That's the problem, Lizzy. I can't..." he blinked and swallowed, flipping back from her eyes to her lips.

He was confusing her to no end. What was she supposed to do with this? She fought the urge to pull her hair out of her head with frustration and instead focused intensely on her breathing. He'd made her incredibly uncomfortable, but she didn't dare show it. She wouldn't dare pull away or back down after cornering him. She felt like she should have said something. Anything. But she feared that any sound out of her mouth would just be a sorry squeal, since she was finding it so hard to stand next to him.

He leaned in close to her ear. "Tell me what you're thinking," his tone was demanding.

She swallowed again, harder. Keeping her mind off pulling that towel off him. "I'm wondering what it is about me that you can't forget."

In an instant, his expression turned dark and he tightened his grip on her arms slightly. He shut his eyes, moving his head to the side, almost regretful. He let something slip. An emotion he couldn't control. Was it anger? She was determined more than ever to find out.

Recovering, he slid his hands down her arms, sending goosebumps through her entire body. He lifted a hand and brushed aside the hair that covered her bruised and sewn temple. He kissed near it so gently, she barely felt the touch. The wordless endearment making her shiver again.

"Everything that makes you—you," he said quietly. His lips teasing around her ear.

She was frozen in place. Couldn't move if she tried. It was as if he was putting her under some spell. "Tell me," she breathlessly asked as he pulled her head back and lightly stroked her neck with his lips.

"How you can be stubborn and cute at the same time. The way you still look at me when I say or do something to make you happy," his lip curved on that one. Then he pulled up and frowned, looking into her eyes, as if he were asking her a question he couldn't understand. "How the thought of losing me could make you lose yourself," his voice cracked, and he pulled away.

Liz frowned at that last one but didn't question it. She was more concerned with his sudden change in mood.

He backed away slowly. "We should get to bed."

She could only nod and wait for him to leave. He turned when he got to the doorstop.

"Would you like me to stay with you tonight?" he asked as if she were a hotel guest.

She suddenly found herself acknowledging that no nightmare can be soothed by forced company. She shook her head without facing him and went to her dresser. When she turned back, he was gone.

CHAPTER 19

MATT

The next morning Matt woke up to some noise in the kitchen. He glanced at the clock on the night table, 7:20. Liz hadn't been up this early since June. He put on his jeans and slipped his arms through a white button-down shirt as he raced down the stairs. He smelled coffee from the living room and frowned as he walked into the kitchen. Liz had laid all the mugs from the cupboard onto the marbled kitchen island. He wasn't sure how long Liz had been staring at them before he walked in. She pulled her eyes off the mugs and glanced at him.

"Hey," she muttered.

"Good morning." He raised both his eyebrows.

There was no forced smile this time when she saw him, no waiting for him to offer her anything, as she had since she'd been home, in her guest-feeling existence.

After a few short seconds, she grabbed a mug that read *It's Going to be a Good One* in gold letters on a plain white background. She held it up for him with a lifted eyebrow.

He shook his head and pursed his lips.

Liz pressed her lips together and stretched her head to the side. "Well, it is now." She placed the other seven mugs back in the cupboard and poured herself a cup of coffee.

Matt watched her for a second and went to the cupboard himself to pull out a teal and black striped short mug. It was the one Liz used the most. One that her mother had given her. He poured a cup for himself and sat on a stool across her on the kitchen island.

Liz avoided meeting his eyes and took a bite of her toast. He didn't question her strange demeanor and sudden cold shoulder. He just sat with her and drank his coffee. She took a sip of her black coffee and met his eyes. After a second, she swallowed it down.

"You don't like it. Why are you drinking it?"

"You're certainly going to be no help in getting my memory back, so I think I'll just take it from here," she replied sternly.

Okay. She was angry. That much he understood. And could guess where it was coming from. "Liz I'm sorry about last night," he leaned over the table, wanting to reach for her then paused and glanced down. "I don't want to take advantage of you when you're—."

Liz stared at him coldly. "I'm not stupid, Matt. I can tell when you're lying to me."

Matt narrowed his eyes at her but didn't argue.

"I am done listening to your pathetic blow offs of why you can't be with me. All I needed is proof, something from you to make me believe that I'm not a stranger in this house. I've learned more about myself from other people than from you." She frowned at him. "Do you even know anything about me?"

He moved around the table to her. "I know *everything* about you." At least he thought he did.

She looked up at him and held his gaze without a blink, then stood and went around the kitchen island to pull a large duffle bag from the floor. "Then why aren't you telling me, why aren't you showing me? Something doesn't feel right. And I'm not sitting back and living this non-existent life with you." She threw the strap over her shoulder and headed into the living room.

Matt leaped and caught up to her by the door. He spun her around, knocking the bag off her shoulder. He caught it before it could fall on her foot.

"Where are you going?" he practically scoffed.

Liz lifted her chin to face him. "I'm checking back into the hospital."

Matt felt himself turning red with anger and took a deep breath to control it. "*This* is your home. Liz, this has all been hard on me too, I just—I need time."

Liz shrugged. "Take all the time you need. I'm going back to see Dr. Tai and see if he can help me." She turned to pull the door open.

Matt had all but one second to calm his anger and frustration so that when he pulled on her arm, it wouldn't be forceful. "Wait, there is something we can do."

Nearly one hour later, they sat in the waiting room outside of the neurology wing of the hospital. It wasn't the same floor Liz had been staying on. It was more open, with a rounded reception desk in the middle of the floor. Each glass door leading to another division of the neuro center. Doctors and nurses raced past each other in a scurry. Well, not exactly the nurses. They mostly appeared to be handling busy work in an *I've got all day* slog, or commenting on each other's new hairdo and what they'd had for breakfast. The doctors, on the other hand, raced door through door, stopping at the reception for only a second to check where they were going next. Every minute counting for their next round of bills. Matt sat back in the chair, waiting for Dr. Tai to emerge from one of the glass doors. He hoped it would be soon, before he changed his mind about this whole thing.

"What are we doing here?" Liz finally asked when it seemed she was going to fall out of her seat with impatience.

Some things seemed to stay with her.

"Waiting for Dr. Tai."

"Why?"

Ignoring his wife's soon to be answered question, Matt stood as Dr. Tai approached the half-moon shaped reception desk then turn to his unexpected visitors.

"Mr. and Mrs. Owen," he stated. The tall man taking large steps toward them. He glanced at Liz and gave her a once over. "What brings you here this morning?"

"Dr. Tai, thank you. I apologize, I realize we didn't have an appointment. But I thought we could try the option we had discussed last week." Matt lowered his head at the doctor, who glared slightly before giving a single nod.

"Please follow me."

He led them to a door at the near end of the hall and leaned in to one of the nurses in the area to mutter something too low to hear. The staff member nodded and walked away.

"Right through here, please." Dr. Tai motioned to a single door that led to a small dark room. The lights flickered on through the sense of motion. A small single bed table lay in the middle, surrounded by monitors, machines, a small wooden desk and a few rolling stools. The room couldn't have been much bigger than an average sized walk-in closet, yet somehow, they all fit.

"I apologize for the small space, unfortunately my usual consult room is occupied and I don't want to be interrupted.

Liz looked uncertain and confused. He was surprised she hadn't asked many questions since they got here.

"Liz," Matt started, taking her hands. "I came to see Dr. Tai a few days ago and he suggested something I was thoroughly against because...well because I thought it would be unfair to put you through this—especially against..." he trailed off.

"What is...this?" Liz questioned.

"Dr. Tai had proposed something that could possibly help you get your—or part—of your memories back."

"Liz," Dr. Tai impatiently interjected. "How much do you know about hypnosis?"

Liz frowned. "Hypnosis? I know what it is, but I don't know how it can help me."

"There are a few factors that go into long or short-term memory loss that doesn't fix itself in a matter of days or hours of the trauma. Since you've yet to have even the faintest memory of who you are or anything about your surroundings, it may be time to consider other obstacles or barricades that are preventing you from recollecting any memories." He paused for a short second and eyed them. "Hypnosis has long been used to help in recalling memories. And it may help guide your mind to discover and confront any barriers, ultimately helping you overcome them. Which has shown to be very effective in getting all if not most memories back."

"You think I am keeping myself from remembering... because of some recent event?"

Matt stiffened in his seat.

"How is that possible? Why would I purposely keep myself from remembering?"

Dr. Tai glanced down and then back at his patient. "Not you, necessarily," he put his hands up as if pushing back. "But Liz might be. I'm not saying physically or actively not letting herself—or you remember. But I am saying that mindfully, Liz may be too shocked or stressed or traumatized by recent events or problems that she is keeping herself in a...shell...so to speak. Leaving her body and bare mind to fend for themselves for some time."

Matt watched Liz process that thought.

"Unfortunately, the longer that Liz chooses to stay locked inside, the harder it may be to come out," the doctor informed.

Matt appreciated the doctor's sympathetic and soft tone. He stepped toward Liz and knelt down to face her. "Liz, I only brought you here because you needed help in remembering and there's only so much I could do."

Liz frowned. "Only so much? You haven't done anything," Liz replied in almost a whisper.

From the corner of his eye, Matt noticed the doctor glance at him.

"Yes, Dr. Tai, let's do this." She pulled her hand away from Matt's grip. "I'm ready," she offered with a nod.

Matt stepped away from the two and moved to the door and pulled his fist against his mouth, breathing hard into it.

"Close your eyes, Liz," Dr. Tai directed.

Liz willingly shut them.

The doctor continued to instruct Liz to shift various parts of her body to ensure even and upright positions. Once he was satisfied, he instructed her breathing and guided her in clearing her mind. Liz obediently followed each tranquilly spoken command.

"Liz, I want you to go to the place just before you opened your eyes in your hospital room. Go back to the seconds before the first flash of light you remember seeing. You're probably going to see blackness, but focus on it and see if another image comes to mind."

After a few short seconds, Liz spoke. "I see other flashes of light. But they're burry."

"What color are they?"

"White, red, umm...maybe yellow."

"What do you feel when you see these lights?"

"I'm...I'm trying not to feel."

Dr. Tai frowned and tilted his head to the side. "What *are* you trying to do?"

"I'm trying to clear my eyes. They're wet."

Matt swallowed and shifted.

"Okay. That's very good. Liz. Now let's try to go back more. What happened before your eyes became wet? Can you go back to the moment before?"

"Yes."

"Is someone with you?"

"Yes."

"What was the last thing you remember saying to this person?"

Liz frowned. "I realized I left it back at the house."

"What was this object you were referring to?"

"My phone."

Matt frowned. Then he turned to the doctor, who met his eyes only to see Matt's impatient expression. He threw his arms in the air and shook his head as if to ask where he was going with this. The doctor responded by holding up his hand to Matt and mouthed the word SLOW. Then continued.

"Did you forget your phone?"

"No," Liz responded. A silent moment went by.

Dr. Tai waited patiently while Matt was confused.

Liz continued. "I left it on purpose."

"Why?" Dr. Tai asked calmly.

"Because I knew he wouldn't call." Liz's expression turned sad and hopeless. Matt's heart ached at the sight. He pulled his eyes off her and stared at the cold hard tiled floor.

"What if someone else called?" Dr. Tai didn't bother asking who she referred to.

"I don't have anyone else," her breathing escalated and a single tear fell down her cheek.

Dr. Tai's head lifted and he straightened his back, moving an inch closer to Liz.

Matt swallowed again, as he tried to release the tightening of his throat. Guilt and agony overpowering him so hard he couldn't see straight. He paced just to regain control. Then stopped when he noticed Dr. Tai glare at him.

The doctor stood from his seat and asked Liz to remain in her thoughts for a moment. He walked up to Matt and motioned for him to step out. Outside the door, he whispered. "If you don't relax, I'm going to have to ask you to wait out here.

"How is working backward relevant?" Matt asked, irritated that his questions were upsetting Liz. It was also not getting down to the core issue that Matt had asked Dr. Tai to look for. "Why can't you just start from the time of the—from when this all started."

"That's not how this works Mr. Owen. I'm starting from the last thing that happened and work my way back as far as I need to. Based on her situation and answers, I decide what my next question is and where I'd like her to go. If she happens to mention that during this accident she lost a necklace she got when she was fifteen, then I might jump to her fifteenth birthday," he paused when Matt shook his head to himself. "I can assure you I know what needs to be done to help Liz and I know how I'd like to get there. If I am to help Liz remember, I need to know facts about her life and where the key events lie in order to help her confront and eventually overcome them."

Matt wanted more than anything to help Liz. He hoped memories would come back to her slowly and from the beginning of her life, like the doctor originally suggested. Then she wouldn't have been shocked or scared when she learned about the more recent events. However, the doctor had a point. They needed to get to the core if Matt wanted to know what caused Liz's memory loss. If it was truly the head trauma alone or if a part of her mind was choosing to stay away because of stress and personal trauma. There was also the other thing that he was sure Liz was still keeping from him. He had asked her about it but got nothing the night at his parents' house. He needed to know what that was. It could mean everything for him. Unless Liz told him, he would never know. This very well could be his only way of finding out.

He looked up at the doctor. "I know where they are," Matt insisted.

Dr. Tai stared at Matt for one moment and let out a breath. "Where would you like for me to take her?"

Matt wasn't sure if taking Liz back to the time leading up to their wedding was right. It may be too stressful. But he needed to know. He swallowed again. "Can you take her back to the week before our wedding? We were in our bedroom. We talked for hours about our life together and plans we had. She had a moment where I lost her for a few seconds. Can you take her back there? I need to know what that was."

The doctor hesitated and then looked judgingly at Matt. "I can't do that without the patient's consent."

Matt glared back at him. "I understand," Matt said simply.

Dr. Tai opened the door to let them back in. He took a seat back across from Liz. He woke her up from her state and she was alert again.

Dr. Tai had explained the scene he wanted to take her back to. Liz seemed intrigued at the memory and looked at her husband for guide.

Matt gave her a small grin and nodded. She turned back and agreed. Within seconds, Liz fell under again.

"Liz," the doctor started again, "I'd like for you to go a little further back in time to before you and Matt were married." He glanced at Matt, unsure. "Say a week or so before. You two are—"

"In his bedroom at his old apartment. We just finished a bottle of wine after dinner and talking about our life together," Liz smiled, "making plans."

Matt looked at her thoughtfully, seeing her happy again, even subconscious, meant everything to him.

"What are you two talking about specifically?"

Eyes still closed, lips still slightly lifted on the corners. "Where we'll live. What recipes to swear by. If we should have one car or two," Liz paused and her smile faded, "Promises of always being honest with each other."

"Okay, that all sounds very nice, Liz. Was what you were saying necessarily what you were thinking at that moment?"

"No," she answered immediately. A moment of silence went by. She opened her mouth but seemed to have trouble getting the words out. "I—" she choked out and then stopped. "I need to..."

"What is it, Liz?" the doctor pressured.

She shook her head vigorously. "I can't do it. I can't, the words, they won't come out."

Dr. Tai focused on his patient, his voice raised slightly. "Liz, can you tell me what that is, what are you trying to say?"

Liz gasped and her breathing escalated. The color from her face drained.

Matt watched, tormented, as the woman he loved was forced to confront herself against her will. His own breathing now matched hers and he felt like ripping his own heart out for letting it get this far.

"Stop," Matt demanded, loudly.

Liz frowned.

"Wake her up. Stop this. I don't want to do this anymore."

"Mr. Owen, we are very close." The doctor insisted, his tone abrupt.

"I don't care. I don't need to know. This isn't helping her. And—and I'm not doing this against her will."

Then the doctor turned red at Matt's slip. "You said this is what she wanted."

"Not like this," Matt said. "Now wake her up."

CHAPTER 20

LIZ

With the simple command of the familiar voice, Liz woke from her subconscious and before the doctor could explain anything to her, Matt grabbed her gently by the arm.

"Can I please speak to you alone?"

Liz jumped to follow Matt out, nerves and eagerness waving through her. "What happened? Did you find anything out? I still don't..."

Matt led her down the hallway until they were alone.

"Liz, I don't think you should do it this way."

"But this was—"

"My idea, I know. But Liz..." He took her hands in his, inhaled a deep breath and looked at her. She searched his eyes for an explanation, a reason for his stopping something that he claimed would help her.

"Liz, I know why you want to do this, because you're not sure about me. Because I haven't proven to you that I am the man you love. The man you belong with and the one who promised to always love and care for you," he started. His tone was urgent and desperate.

She swallowed and looked down, wanting deeply to believe him.

He tightened the grip on her hands and took a step closer to her. "Lizzy, I promise you—this *is* where you belong.

With me. Please give me another chance to prove it to you. I know I can."

"I don't understand, why did you stop him? This could be it, Matt," Liz didn't want to go back based on his word.

He shook his head but held her gaze. "No, I don't think it is. I think I can do better. I can help you remember everything in the way that I want you to remember, Lizzy," he paused. "Please come back home with me. Let me remind you who we are together."

Liz's face softened with nearly every word. But when he was done and waiting, she glanced down, hesitating and then looking back at Dr. Tai, who had emerged from the small room and watched them from a distance.

"You said the same thing to me when I first left this place with you. Why should I trust you now?"

Matt was still for a moment, as if he was silently answering her question. It seemed to her for a fraction of a second that he was going to tell her, but then, to her disappointment, he hesitated.

"You just need to trust me, Liz. I can promise you, you're my only concern now. Helping you and healing you."

Liz let out a loud sigh. She needed more.

"That's not good enough. I'm going through with this." She pulled out of his grasp and was halfway down the corridor when she froze at his words.

"The figurine in the emerald green dress on the piano," Matt called after her, "It was a gift I'd brought you from Ireland." Liz didn't turn around, but kept listening. "I had gone off to Ireland after grad school—just as you and I were—well, getting serious and it was time for that next step," he paused. "When I saw that figurine...with her long brown hair and beautiful green gown, I thought it looked just like you, and how I wished you were with me. It's when I realized I never wanted to be without you," he paused and she turned. He threw his arms up. "There was really no sentimental value to it, Liz. It just always meant a lot to you, that thing. Because in your eyes, it's what brought me back to you."

She stood in place, afraid that any move, in either direction would make him stop.

He laughed lightly. "That's why you're drawn to it now, your heart is telling you to trust it."

Liz flushed. "How did you know..."

"Because it moves a little bit every day," he said, with a small smile.

Liz studied him for a moment, appreciating the way he openly let her in on what he'd noticed. She took a small step, but hesitated, which made Matt take a few steps towards her.

"And I never told you exactly how we met and fell in love, did I?" He stopped inches from her and proceeded to tell her the details of how they came to fall in love. From the first bonfire, down to the spare key under her mat.

Liz narrowed her eyes at the new openly in love man standing before her holding out his hand.

*   *   *

After clearing the dishes of the romantic meal he'd made for them, Matt joined Liz on the couch with refilled glasses of her favorite merlot.

"Where were we?" he asked, bouncing down next to her.

"You were just telling me—no sorry—reminding me," as he had insisted they call it, "about the time I would wake up at five a.m. every morning for a week to deviously dump all the coffee in both lounge rooms in the dorms until they started stocking coffee that didn't taste like mud."

"Oh, yes," he grinned. "You said it was a necessary evil. Then you made me have everyone on my side of the dorms sign a 'petition'—I lost respect from a lot of people that week."

Liz laughed whole-heartedly out loud. Freer than she had with her own brother. This was different. Being with Matt now felt real. "I can't believe you let me do that," she wiped at a tear. "You didn't go running for the nearest exit?"

Matt smiled at her thoughtfully, "Oh Lizzy, there isn't much you could do that would make me turn away from you."

As his words were spoken, Liz thought she caught a glimpse of doubt and hurt in his eyes. It could have just been her imagination, but it was the same look she'd seen on him before. She didn't have far back to remember, so memorizing every expression and emotion from him was everything to her.

Liz put her glass down, suddenly losing appetite for any more alcohol.

"Something wrong?" he asked her, frowning.

"I don't know yet."

Matt nodded.

"I think I've had enough stories for one night, though." Liz stood, "Thank you for dinner and for tonight," she smiled down at him and turned.

As she reached the stairs, Matt grabbed and spun her to face him. His face nearly an inch from hers.

"Liz," he breathed.

Her eyes found his and then dropped to his lips. She'd been longing to feel them again since he'd kissed her before leaving for his parent's beach house. Whatever happened there to change his mind when he got home, was something she figured she'd never learn.

He traced his fingers up her arms, sending chills down her spine. She inhaled deeply, trying desperately to control herself. To resist wanting more from him. Hoping that he didn't feel like she needed this, she backed up two more steps.

Following her, he kept his hands around her waist and pinned her against the wall, facing him.

She let out a low whimper with the need for him to follow through. His hands traced up her shoulders and neck and cupped her face. He gave her one last hungry look before crushing her lips with his. She let him devour her for a mere few seconds before fully engaging in the kiss herself, giving him all she had.

"Tell me this is what you want," he murmured against her lips.

"For as long as I can remember," she replied honestly.

He smiled against her lips and slowly pulled them up the stairs. Halfway up they crashed and laughed, only parting lips for a second. Finally making it up the stairs, Matt led her into their dimly lit bedroom.

For a brief moment, before he guided her onto the bed, Liz glanced to the spot in the room remembering the night before when Matt had outwardly rejected her. Knowing there had been something dark in his eyes, something he was hiding. Something he was *still* hiding; she was sure of it. Something that had to do with *her*. It would be foolish to think it didn't. It was only visible when he looked directly at her. When she'd advanced on him and challenged him to be with her the way a husband should.

In the midst of her thoughts, she felt his warm, gentle hand slip under her shirt and unclasp her bra. It was so smooth and deft, like someone who'd done the same thing with her a thousand times. But contrary to what she'd told him down on the stairwell, she wasn't ready for this.

She needed to know what it was that rested behind those doubting eyes.

After a few more heated exchanges of kisses, she reluctantly pushed him off her.

He pulled back with his eyes wide. "I'm sorry. I shouldn't have just—"

"No, it's fine. I am just...I just wanted to know..." she trailed off. It wasn't that she hesitated to ask him something, it was that she wasn't sure what there was to ask.

But the way he looked at her right now, there was no doubt in her mind that he wanted her. Why fight it? Why question it? "It's nothing," she insisted.

When he just stared at her for a few seconds, giving her time to change her mind, she decided he needed more convincing. Pulling herself up, she pulled her shirt off, letting the bra he unclasped a moment ago fall off her shoulders.

"Can you remind me how I like it?" she whispered in his ear.

He let out a soft growl and pulled her against his chest. Her pulse raced and she barely felt his hand glide up her skirt. He kissed her with so much force, she was going to lose her mind. He lifted her and pinned her against the headboard. Pulling away for only a moment to slide off his pants and remove his shirt, he met her back against the board, kissing her furiously. She hadn't realized his hands were tightly holding her thighs in place until both hands started moving slowly up her skirt. His right hand pressed firmly against her back while the other teased her with strokes.

"Does it matter how you liked it before?" he whispered back, softly blowing in her ear. "Tell me what you want now." He kept stroking her slowly, but wouldn't go further. Not until she answered him. That was clear.

She opened her eyes and noticed a slight smirk as he watched her need build. "I want you to stop playing," she murmured as she lowered herself into his hold.

Instantly his smirk turned into a wide grin as he pushed two fingers into her, pulling her deeper with the hand that still rested on her lower back.

CHAPTER 21

MATT

Matt watched Liz sleep soundly next to him. He hadn't realized how much he missed her until now. The last time they were intimate was at his parents' house, the night he'd found out about them and he'd returned drunk after spending hours at the Tavern. He swallowed hard with the memory of feeling like he'd forced her, even though she was willing and almost desperate for him that night. The memory of asking her to close her eyes as he approached and handled her just to see if she trusted him, sent an invisible knife through his heart.

He tried to replay the night. Every inch of her he touched. Not just where but how forceful and demanding. Nothing stuck out at him, he'd always been gentle with her, but he cringed, regardless.

What if she didn't like it and endured it to prove something to him? He'd never imagined putting her through that, or anyone for that matter. It wasn't who he was.

Then again, that night, he didn't know who he was married to either. The stranger he thought he knew and trusted. The woman who had done the unthinkable and then went on to lie about it for years.

He fought the urge to throw off the covers and storm off. He couldn't confuse and hurt her like that again. This innocent woman needed him. Today, after they'd returned from the hospital, she reminded him of the woman he met years ago. It was almost like their first date all over again. Getting to know each other. Except in this case, she was getting to know both of them.

Matt decided Liz wasn't ready to start getting her memories back. There had been too much tragedy and trauma in her life for her to remember all at once. He had to help her get to know him better first so she could trust him and feel safe with him, then the memories wouldn't be so bad.

Then how is she going to feel when you finally tell her it's over?

The constant inner reminder of the fact that he never got the chance to tell her he couldn't forgive or get past her betrayal had become a nagging thought as well.

Somehow, when the time was right, they'd talk. But first, he needed to take care of her. And she needed tender care. Before they fell asleep, Matt had asked Liz about her nightmare. She'd finally opened up about it and it nearly killed him when she finished. She had said it was "terrible."

Matt determined it was damn near horrific.

The sub-conscious human mind was becoming more of a phenomenon to him as he remembered her description of the car accident. The blinding headlights, shattered glass, the dead parents—and what struck him the most—the unfazed husband who stared at her as she bled out. That wasn't exactly how she described it, but the picture was well painted, and it was the exact definition of a nightmare.

In her dream, she was alone. Even her husband, who had "survived" the accident, didn't seem to care that she was hurt and needed him. She was in every sense of the word—alone.

He rubbed his temples to soothe the growing headache as he continued torturing himself, wondering how much of his "empty look" in her dream resembled the look he'd given her when she took his keys and left the house. A shiver went down his spine. He couldn't believe he'd left her that morning to go work on a boat!

Liz broke into his thoughts when she shifted closer to him and he leaned in to wrap an arm around her. Her warm body felt right under his touch, and he could feel, if not see on her rested features, that she was content in his arms. Perhaps he would get some sleep that night after all.

CHAPTER 22

LIZ

Liz poured a steamy cup of coffee for herself. She insisted to keep trying all the things she'd been known to do and enjoy before her accident. To feel as much like herself as possible. The doctor had given her a comparison of imagining that she had walked to work the same way for five years, and then one day decided to choose a different route. "Why would you do anything that wouldn't be familiar to you, even if you don't like it?" Dr. Tai had explained.

Liz sat on one of the bar stools along the kitchen island as she pondered other advice and guidance that her doctor had given her. He seemed to be the only one who wanted her to get her memory back. Now thinking about her own husband's unwillingness, previous to last night, to help her remember anything at all. Were they having problems? A scarier thought entered Liz's mind. Was there a pending separation and he'd only shown up at the hospital because he was her only contact?

No.

It couldn't be.

There was her brother Marcus.

Then again, Marc didn't seem like he was itching for Liz to get her memory back either. He wouldn't even go through family albums with her without clamming up.

What was her only known family hiding from her?

Suddenly Liz remembered the hypnosis from the night before. If the purpose of it was to help Liz get her memory back, why did Matt suddenly stop it? What was she on the verge of saying or remembering that Matt didn't want?

Nothing made sense. However, the coffee was beginning to taste a lot better to her. Maybe the good doctor was onto something.

Was he good?

On the drive home from the hospital yesterday after Matt had vowed to be the man she needed, and followed through, Liz wondered what Matt and Dr. Tai had initially planned. And why was it suddenly pulled to a halt? The doctor certainly did not seem pleased when they left. He seemed irritated.

Liz put her mug down abruptly, deciding she needed to know why.

An hour later, Liz sat and waited in the same spot where she had the day before with her husband. The same nurses and technicians that had once fussed over her incessantly as a patient, now flew by her as though she were invisible. She had asked the same receptionist if Dr. Tai was in and if she could speak with him. After a quick nod, she was directed to the same seating area. After thirty minutes, she began to get impatient and asked again. Only for a generic excuse for the delay and point to have a seat. After another few minutes, Liz turned at a familiar voice. Only this time knowing it wasn't quite her husband's voice, as she had thought the last time she heard it.

Ben stood at the same reception desk, demanding to see what the hospital had submitted to his insurance company.

"Of course, Mr. Owen. Please have a seat and we'll call you when it's ready."

Ben gathered his papers and turned toward the waiting area. Liz quickly turned away.

"Liz?" he called.

She turned, trying her best to act surprised to see him. "Hi, Ben."

"Is everything okay?" His voice full of concern as he approached her.

"What? Oh no, yes. Everything is fine. I'm just here to see my doctor."

He looked around. Looking almost annoyed. "Matt didn't come with you?"

"No," she said casually, hoping it wouldn't lead to any questions.

Ben shook his head. "He should be here with you. I'll call him."

"No don't. He...I don't want him to know I came here today," her eyes silently pleading with his.

Ben looked at Liz for a moment. His face unreadable. "Can I ask why?"

Liz turned. "There's just something I'm confused about."

He took a seat next to her and seemed to want to press further. But Liz could see he was hesitating. "You know, Liz," he started after a long moment. "I know you don't remember this, but you and I are actually pretty close." He seemed to be waiting for her to respond. "If you ever need anything, don't hesitate. Please."

Liz watched him. He seemed so sincere. She wondered how a sincere man like him could be married to a seemingly unsympathetic person like Megan.

After a breath, Liz began, "I was just here with Matt yesterday. We came to see Dr. Tai, my neurologist and," she hesitated, "apparently my hypnotist."

Ben's frowned. "Hypnosis? Is that a way of helping you get your memories back?"

"Sort of. They want to use it to see where the factors lie." Liz went into the short version of what the doctor and Matt had told her and what happened in the room, including Matt's eagerness to call it. She stopped when Ben's expression appeared more enraged than curious.

"Maybe I shouldn't be discussing this with you," she said softly.

He seemed to snap out of it. "Maybe. But Liz, I also think that if you're having doubts about your treatment, you should talk to Matt. Clearly, him stopping midway is bothering you and you should ask him why." He looked around the hospital and then at his hands, which were twined tightly together. "Nothing good comes of keeping secrets," Ben added.

Liz didn't realize she had been staring at Ben after he said those last words, until he looked away uncomfortably.

"You've said that to me before," she said in a dazed whisper.

Ben returned her gaze. "I did? When?"

She shook her head. She heard him say that before. And it was significant when said, but for the life of her, she couldn't remember when, where or why. She just felt the tension in her heart from the last time she'd heard him say it.

"Listen, I'm going to pick up some papers here, but how about I take you home and you can think about what I said." He stood. "Besides, these doctors tend to charge a fortune for a 5-minute conversation and I just hate to stand back and watch that happen," he said with a wink.

Liz nodded.

When he returned, he reached out his hand and she took it, standing to her feet. Perhaps he was right. She should talk to Matt.

"I know you don't believe this now, but you can trust him. More than anyone else." He glanced at the slew of hospital staff bustling about. "Especially anyone here."

CHAPTER 23

MATT

Tuesday morning Matt packed a small cooler with sparkling white wine, two plastic wine glasses, and an assortment of cheese and fruit. He was taking Liz to her favorite beach, hoping it would help relieve some of the tension he knew she still felt days after their spontaneous visit to Dr. Tai. Matt had ignored the many calls from the doctor following that day. He wasn't ready for what he was being *strongly encouraged* to do.

Mr. Owen, if you don't want to bring Elizabeth in for treatment, I strongly encourage that you help her in retrieving her memories in a slow but efficient manner with honesty, no matter how hard it may be. The downfall of not doing so could be very dangerous and lead to serious mental setbacks if her memories start flooding back negatively before she's ready. Please call me so we can discuss this in more detail. Matt replayed the last voicemail in his head as he pulled two towels from the linen closet in the hallway and walked back into their bedroom.

Liz stood in her purple one-piece swimsuit that hugged her curvy upper body while revealing the rest of her flawless skin. Her long dark waves fell over her shoulders and ran just below her elbow. She froze in place when he'd opened the door and just stared at her. She held a pair of white sandals.

"I-I'm sorry, this is mine right," she asked, with a crooked smile, pointing to the swimsuit, which had not only caught his eye, but also his tongue in this throat. He mentally shook his head. Why was he acting as if he'd never seen her in a swimsuit?

You're just admiring what you're going to miss.

He ignored the small part of his subconscious. "You could borrow it," he smiled back and winked. He walked up to the bed and tossed the two towels into the beach bag, and Liz added the sandals.

"What's wrong with the ones you're wearing?" he asked, noticing the purple flip flops she had on.

"Oh, well, if I get sand in these, I'll change into the cleaner shoes before getting in your car. I don't want to make a mess, you seem to keep it so clean."

She was kidding right?

Matt smiled and thought for a moment how he could really get used to this Liz. He shook his head. "You don't need to worry about our car," he told his wife as she slipped on a white knitted dress, revealing the purple fabric underneath. He grabbed the bag and her hand and led them out of the room. Leaning into her on the way down, he whispered, "in fact, a lot dirtier stuff has happened in that car...and in many of our previous vehicles."

Liz flushed and grinned at him. The morning was off to a good start.

*   *   *

Matt tossed the last piece of cheese into his mouth. Sitting up from his towel, he grabbed what was left of the wine from the cooler and held it up to Liz.

"One more?"

"No, no. Any more and you'd be carrying me back to the car."

Matt glanced around at their belongings. "I could manage it all," he noted before cocking his head to study her upper body, "the swimsuit might be a bit too much though, we'll have to leave it behind."

Liz threw her head back, laughing. "Is that how dirty things end up happening in your car?

Matt couldn't help his wide grin. The sound of her laughter continuing to fill him in all the right places. "Yes, I bring you to the middle of nowhere, get you nice and buzzed to the point where you can't walk, and then trick you into taking your clothes off."

"Okay. Let's clean up," Liz insisted, sitting up and dusting the sand off her long legs.

Once they were all packed and on their way back to the car, Matt stopped and turned to her. "Hey, why don't we stay on the beach a while longer." He pulled a bag off her shoulder. "I'll drop these off at the car."

"That sounds great," she smiled up at him. "Wait," she took a step closer and pulled her pale pink skirt from the beach bag. "I'll wait here."

Matt ran the towels and basket back to his SUV. He hadn't brought his phone with him to the beach. He was avoiding any and all devices while spending time with Liz. She hadn't been carrying her cell phone around, insisting she didn't need it. Other than Marcus, Matt was her only connection and the only person who would call, so what would be the point? He took a peek at it from the window and decided to give it a quick check before heading back.

Nothing other than a text from Ben. The last person he wanted to hear from.

We need to talk. Please call me.

Like hell they did.

The only thing Matt would want to say to his brother at the moment, was that no thanks to him, he was beginning to trust Liz again. Matt threw the phone back in the car and looked up, sighing. Then again, it was easy to trust someone who is practically a brand new, innocent person with no memory of the way she'd hurt and betrayed him.

He found Liz standing closer to shore than where he'd left her, raising her knee-high skirt even higher to see her feet touch the waves that were slowly flowing in and out.

Making his way across the warm sand until he reached her, he placed both hands around her waist, making her jump. Matt grinned at her. "Sorry."

Liz shook her head playfully. "I don't think you are." She pulled his hand into hers and looked up at him. "Which way?"

Matt glanced to his left. "This way."

They strolled for nearly an hour and talked about what Matt had subconsciously called "safe conversation." Consisting primarily on funny stories from their past together and then a few non-past related items, like what his parents are like and how often they stay at their summer home. Liz seemed to be particularly interested in his family. Matt guessed it was probably because she didn't have much of her own. He wished more than anything, that he had more to tell her about her parents, but he barely knew them before their accident. Which tragically would have been the same way he'd lost Liz if she weren't so lucky.

It was hard to feel sad at that moment when he was having such an amazing time with his wife. One he'd missed over the past few weeks. One he didn't remember chatting this much with since before they were married.

Lost in thought, he hardly noticed that Liz seemed pretty far in her own thoughts. He wondered what he could say to make her open up to him. To trust him. He didn't blame her for being distant, not after he'd been giving her mixed signals. He stopped just as the sun was starting to set far off in the horizon.

"Lizzy," he grabbed both her hands in his, "thank you for spending today with me," he whispered. "I know it's been...difficult and confusing living with me, but..." he trailed off for a moment and swallowed, ensuring that this is something he wanted to promise her. "I promise, I'm going to make things right."

Before she could respond with anything, he bent down and kissed her lightly, holding her soft lips, savoring them. Why he thought he needed to, he couldn't tell.

She pulled away slowly and gazed off at the setting sun. "It's so beautiful here. Did we come here a lot?" she asked after a moment.

"We did, and still do." Matt wasn't exactly lying. They did pass by this beach quite often when in town and when the weather was nice for strolling through the nearby shops, but they hadn't had picnics or strolled on any beach since their honeymoon. But if he'd told her that, she'd just ask why now, and "guilt" wasn't exactly the answer he wanted to give her. "You'll start getting memories back soon, Liz, I know it. I'm going to help you."

Who are you trying to convince with that last one? That annoying voice again.

She looked down and he noticed what looked almost like a grimace on her face. He couldn't imagine what could have upset her. Did she remember something? Was she doubting his sincerity?

"Liz, is something wrong?"

She glanced up at him tentatively and then focused on the sand beneath her. Then finally spoke in a quiet voice. "Not exactly, well, speaking of memories, there's something I should tell you."

Matt's heart skipped two beats as he braced himself. Had she had a memory? What if the first thing she remembered was the thing Matt feared most? Their fight the night before the accident? The night she'd spent with his brother? How would he explain that? "You had a memory?"

There must have been twenty possible things that passed through his head before she finally looked him in the eye and spoke.

"Something like that." The light wind was pulling dark strands of her hair onto her face. Her long eyelashes blinking them away as she tried to focus on him.

"Why didn't you say something? What was it?" He knew he shouldn't press, but he just had to know what it was. He couldn't place a finger on the look on her face. Guilt? Confusion? Maybe both?

She took a breath, her eyes scattering a two-foot radius that surrounded where they'd stood. "The other day, I went to see Dr. Tai..." Liz started, glancing up for his reaction. "It's just, things changed so fast between us and I wanted to know if it was because of something I said while I was under the hypnosis." She looked back at him, "You were so eager to call it off and then had done a complete three-sixty...it...it made me wonder..." she glanced away, "if there was something you didn't want me to know...or remember."

Matt blinked. He tried to think of something to say, to explain and reassure, but the truth was, he couldn't blame her for questioning it. In fact, it was definitely something *his* Liz would have done.

He watched her waiting eyes for a moment, as if needing reassurance that it was okay to continue. He cleared his throat. "Is there more?"

CHAPTER 24

LIZ

Though he tried to hide it, Liz immediately noticed her husband's pupils dilate and his jaw tighten the second she mentioned that his brother showed up. She frowned. She would have sworn that telling him that Ben found her there would be a relief. That she wasn't alone. But then remembered the thick tension between the brothers back in her hospital room. Surely what she was about to tell him would help.

She held up her hands, instinctively. "I didn't ask him to come, he was there to question Megan's medical bill."

Matt waited. She quickly scanned for breathing patterns and facial expressions of anger, but only noted his broad chest kick and tighten. She was highly cognizant and weary of his strongly held-back emotions.

She continued regardless, "I told him about our visit to Dr. Tai," she paused, "and that I'd come back to see him... on my own...for answers." She glanced up and swallowed hard, forcing herself to continue when he spiked it up a notch with his hard glare.

Why was he being like this?

"Anyway, he convinced me that I should go home and talk to you about any of my doubts." Which she was now doubting. "Even if they have to do with you, that we should talk them through."

Matt glanced around them, as if unsure what he should say or do.

"Are you mad?"

"You mentioned something about a memory?" her husband reminded, barely looking at her.

"It wasn't really a memory, it was just something that Ben said that...or warned rather."

Matt's brow lifted slightly.

"He said, 'nothing good comes of keeping secrets', and I...I know I've heard it before. From *him*. Only, it was important when he said it and...there was tension..." Liz turned her head down, the memory so unclear. It was just something she knew she'd heard him say before. And the first time he'd said it, it had made Liz terrified, or maybe angry? She couldn't decide, but there were strong feelings behind it. She looked up at her very still and silent husband.

"Matt?"

"Your first memory...was of my brother?" His eyes narrowed.

Liz held up her hands for the second time during that conversation, and placed them on his chest. "It's nothing like that." Liz wasn't even sure why she had to say that, but it seemed appropriate judging by the hurt look on his face. "He just said something I may have heard him say before, I'm sure it was just déjà vu or something." She shrugged, "Anyway, he didn't remember, so it probably didn't happen." Liz didn't understand her need to convince Matt that it was no big deal and that it was probably not a real memory. But she knew it was. And based on the response she got from both of them, she was determined to find out what was behind that piece of advice the older brother had given her. On more than one occasion.

Matt seemed to snap out of his daze and took a breath. "Did he say anything else?" His tone more conversational now.

She wasn't convinced.

And she wasn't having any more of this. Not today. Not when things had been going so well and she'd started feeling more at home with him. She shook her head in response. "I'm sorry, I should have come to you with my doubts."

Matt blinked. "I...um...I can't blame you." He watched the ocean waves for a moment. He obviously found comfort there, because when he looked back at her, kindness and sincerity gleamed in his eyes. "You're lost now. You have questions and I...haven't been very good at answering them. I guess I just don't know how to convince someone that they belong with me." He smiled weakly.

Liz blushed as he pushed away the strands of hair from her face and tucked them behind her ear.

"Are you always this understanding?"

Matt looked up from her and cocked his head to the side. "Not always." He looked at her again and smiled, his eyes reflecting the orange rays from the sun that had nearly set behind her. "Let's go home."

* * *

"Morning," she practically sang out as Matt walked into the kitchen the next morning. She moved around the spacious area between their island and the sink in her short white bathrobe. She'd typically get fully dressed before coming downstairs, but since she had no plans, what would be the point? That and she'd admittedly started to feel more at home since her breakthrough with Matt. She preferred honesty and wanted to keep it that way going forward. "You were up early."

He wore gray sweat shorts and a white fitted t-shirt. She immediately noticed the sweat stains and bare glossy features. His eyes were a shinier green and overall, he looked much more...toned.

"I went for a run," he said breathlessly. He wasn't panting, but his chest still heaved slightly. He brushed past her and her cheeks flamed.

"You should ask me to go with you next time."

He poured his coffee carefully and yet nearly spilled some as he choked a laugh. "Oh, Lizzy. You don't run."

Her mouth dropped comically. "Last time I checked, I didn't lose my legs in this accident," she placed her arms at her sides with determination, "so tomorrow morning, I'll be coming with you!"

Matt pursed his lips.

Annoyed, she waved an arm at him. "That's okay, you can pretend you don't know me if I turn out to be a hot mess out there."

"It is going to be hot, but you won't be a mess, because you won't get very far. You never exercise." Matt pressed his lips together and crinkled his nose, no doubt imagining her fall from weakened knees three blocks into the run.

"I'll be fine!" she insisted, closing the cupboard after grabbing the teal and black striped mug.

CHAPTER 25

MATT

Matt froze. She had grabbed *her* mug. Her favorite. He frowned as he turned back the wheels to five seconds ago to see if she sought it out or if it had been the easiest to grab. He couldn't place the mug, but he remembered her scanning for a quick second.

Matt shook his head lightly. *The sub-conscious human mind.*

"What?" Liz questioned.

"I was just thinking, you might wake up with your memory back, sore as hell the next morning, and you'll kill me for letting you run two miles with me."

"So we'll start slow," she shrugged, her enthusiasm unfading, even at the mention of distance. She smiled at him as if to reassure that she wasn't backing down.

Her smile was infectious.

Not once in the past two weeks had she lost her beauty, but she looked especially alluring today. He couldn't place if it was the calm, content and trusting look she'd had since they'd left the beach last night, or if there was something different she'd done with her hair that morning. A complete transformation from woman he'd spent the last week with. Her soulless persona had been replaced with a joyful, humorous and magnificent individual that he remembered falling deeply for years ago. He made a mental note not to screw up before approaching to tuck her hair behind her ear.

"Okay," he said softly. A natural tone she brought out in him when she was this close. He started to head out. "Oh hey, just be sure to eat light today, you know, since I'm probably going to be carrying you back home tomorrow," he winked at Liz's unamused look before darting out.

*　*　*

Matt sat in his office between meetings with the school Board and his department. He needed a quiet hour, more than anything. And he was still annoyed from yet another voicemail from his mother asking for him and Liz to come for the weekend. A weekend at the beach house, which Ben and Megan had apparently already agreed to. All the more reason Matt wasn't going to go—or take Liz to for that matter.

He couldn't risk losing it in front of Liz. No. He wouldn't take her there. Not now. Not when things have been going great with them. Liz was trusting him more and more every day. He hated keeping some things from her, but saw no other way. He had to protect her.

And give himself more time.

A vision of Lizzy came into his mind as she pleaded with him back in that guest room about why she lied to him all these years.

No. This was different. This was pure protection for someone he loved.

The knock on his door snapped him out of his intense thoughts. He pulled it open and frowned. "Megan?"

Megan nodded and gave him a small grin as she brushed past him to get through the door. "Sorry to bother you at work."

Matt didn't try to cover his annoyance as he closed the door reluctantly, "What do you want Megan?"

"Francis sent me. She said this is your last chance before they go to Liz about this weekend."

"Geez," Matt threw his hands in the air and stormed across the room, to his window. "Would you all just give it a rest?" He turned to Megan. "Besides, I hear you don't have to threaten me to pay a visit to your sister-in-law." He raised his eyebrows.

Megan cocked her head. "Don't worry, I didn't tell her any details of our car ride."

He shrugged. "What's there to hide? You said you two were laughing on the drive home," There was more to the story. He knew it by the way Megan tensed and kicked him out that day in the hospital.

"Yup," Megan nodded slowly.

"What else happened Megan? What are you leaving out? I know she didn't crash from laughing to tears."

Megan glanced down and to her left before lifting her head proudly. "How would you know, maybe I'm that funny."

Matt shot her a hard look, "Wait, that's it, isn't it? Was she crying?" Of course, she was crying. That's why the traffic lights and everything in front of her was blurry. That's why it was "raining" in her dream.

"It's none of your business," Megan said quietly.

"Are you kidding? It's no body's business *but* mine," he exploded.

Megan glanced at her watch. Typical.

"Let's be honest Meg, you've never been the type to *protect* anyone. Whatever you're not telling me, it's something *you* did."

Megan glared at him with disbelief. "You said a crapload of things to upset her, no one's attacking you," she barked back.

Matt took a deep breath. "I'm sorry Megan, I not trying to attack you. I just want to know what happened."

Megan's expression turned dark and remorseful. But she was a businesswoman and never let her emotions out for too long. She lifted her head again. "Fine, I'll tell you. But there's a condition."

Matt leaned in as if he didn't hear correctly. "A condition?" Then held his hands up, giving in. He knew how Megan worked. She'd never give in unless she felt like she'd won somehow. Even though this was no win or lose matter. "Fine."

"Ben's been trying to reach you—"

"Out of the question—"

"Let me finish. I'm not asking you to call or even talk to Ben. But Francis is really upset that you've been ignoring her. I came here to ask you to come to the beach house this weekend, and bring Liz. We all want to see her."

Matt chuckled, but he hated where this was going.

"Obviously, if Liz doesn't feel comfortable, then you don't have to come, but if she wants to, you can't keep her from coming," Megan paused. "We're her family too." She kept her gaze on him, undoubtedly to make sure he understood her terms.

Matt shut his eyes and rubbed his temples. "Okay."

"I know I said I didn't remember, but...I remember it as if it were moments ago." She strolled around the space, twining her fingers. Her voice was casual, but he could hear the slightest shake in it. "I said something along the lines of 'I told you so', which Liz expected and made fun of, and although we *were* in fact laughing to tears, I knew hers were...sad."

Matt caught a glimpse of Megan's sympathy and wanted to tell her never to feel sorry for his wife. But he withheld, reminding himself she needed to tell him what happened.

"That's when I said it. Something stupid…I wasn't even thinking…"

"Megan," Matt pressed.

"I said I really hope Matt does forgive you, because I can't imagine having this much fun with anyone else," she blurted.

Matt frowned and glared at her.

"I mean I didn't even think anything of it. It was a meaningless statement." Megan added defensively. "It wasn't until I saw the look on her face—the idea of you being with someone else—just downright plagued her."

Meaningless statement that nearly killed his wife. The woman who had cared so deeply for him that she lost control and then her mind at the thought of losing him to someone else. Regardless of losing her parents in recent years, contact with her brother, and having to live with a mistake she made out of grief, Liz still managed to be a full spirited and bright person. Her heart, still wide open despite tragedy in her adult life. She managed to keep six and seven-year old's happy and excited to learn every day. Yet one stupid comment from this woman and she'd nearly lost it all.

"Is that when she crashed?" His voice coarse.

"Not exactly. She started crying a fresh set of tears and asked me to call you guys—I guess to distract me from feeling sorry for her."

He knew it. It was the blurred vision that made her crash. As much as he wanted to blame Megan for it, it wasn't entirely her fault. Maybe not at all.

It was unquestionably his.

Megan glanced at Matt. No longer carrying the same *I'll outsmart you any day* look on her face that she was when they were making their deal. Now she just looked defeated and remorseful.

Matt turned away from her and walked to his window. It was time for his end of the deal. And for Megan to leave. "Tell my mother we'll be there on Saturday."

CHAPTER 26

LIZ

Matt wasn't kidding when he said it was going to be hot. A scorching ninety-two degrees. He also wasn't joking when he told her she doesn't run. There had been no sign of any jogging clothes in the closet or dresser. But there was no way she was backing out. She had found a pair of black and silver leggings and a pink sports bra. She met Matt downstairs, and they both downed a cold bottle of water before heading out.

After jogging for nearly twenty minutes, Liz was out of breath and sweating. Feeling the strain in her calves, she slowed down and took a deep breath before halting and resting her hands on her knees.

Matt stopped and turned back to her, jogging in place. "Oh come on, we just started."

She glanced up, and as expected, found his "I told you so" smirk. "I didn't...say...I was stopping," Liz rasped out.

"Okay, good. We've got another thirty minutes ahead, and then we'll turn back."

Liz squinted up at him, wondering at what point he'd start to break a sweat. With her hands still on her knees, she managed to get more words out. "And *then* we'll turn back?" She stood, rolling her eyes. "Okay. You win. I can't do this. I'm not even comfortable in these clothes." She motioned her arms down her body.

A slow smile crept up his face. Matt stopped his jog and reached for her hand. "Come on." He walked her ahead about half a block before they reached a small coffee shop. It was incredibly tiny, with only a narrow entrance door and small window for ordering. There were two small round metal tables outside with matching chairs.

Matt approached the closed window. A young kid with strawberry blond hair and overly tanned skin opened it. Liz breathed in the incredibly cool burst of air that quickly emerged from the small window. "Two lemonades, please."

"Two lemonades." The guy repeated before disappearing behind the counter.

Matt turned to Liz and brushed away a few soaking strands of hair from her face.

"We taking a break?" Liz asked, glancing at the chairs.

"Not exactly," he turned back to the window. "Besides you wouldn't want to sit on those piping hot metal chairs right now."

The kid reappeared with the drinks. "Five dollars."

"Thanks, Tyler."

Liz eyed the pale cool drink in her husband's hands before he handed her one. She took a long sip of the sweet and tangy liquid refreshment. It wasn't until she gulped down her second long sip that she noticed Matt grinning at her.

"This is really good," Liz inhaled deep for air, "but I don't think this is going to help me run back another twenty minutes."

He flashed her an all-knowing smile, his eyes a bright green in the sunlight. He put an arm around her, and she leaned into his warm, solid body. "We're not running. Come on," he nodded ahead, "our place is around the corner, just a five-minute walk or so."

She glanced back to the direction they came from. "What? We just made a huge circle?" Liz narrowed her eyes at him. "You really had no faith in me."

Matt raised an eyebrow.

"Hmm." She held out her hand to him.

Liz took another long refreshing sip and looked around the neighborhood. She liked the town they lived in. It was clean and just the right amount of neighborhood bustling. The streets they jogged mainly had cookie cutter townhomes resembling the one they lived in. The business section of the neighborhood seemed small, primarily consisting of small shops like a cafe, deli, barber shop, pet shop, and the ice-cream and lemonade boutique.

"Did you grow up here?"

"Huh?"

"Are you from this town?"

"Oh, no. My brother and I were born and raised on Long Island, not in the house they live in now, but nearby."

Liz nodded and took a longer sip of her half empty drink. "So what was the occasion for us visiting that weekend?"

Something dark appeared in Matt's expression, quickly shifting from cool to cold.

"It was the Fourth of July weekend," he answered blankly and stared ahead.

Liz's eyes popped and she automatically shined a smile. "Oh, how nice." Liz frowned. "I'm sorry I missed the fireworks."

"Oh, you didn't miss much, my dad's fireworks are nothing to be impressed about, he gets the discounted version and it never lasts longer than fifteen minutes or so."

This had been the first time it appeared that her husband was rambling. It confused her at first, but then after listening to him for another moment, she smiled at the presumption that he didn't want her to feel like she'd missed out. She smiled at his thoughtfulness.

"Must have been a disappointing weekend."

"Uneventful, I'd say." Matt pursed his lips and cocked to the side.

Liz nodded in response. "Except for...losing your wife," she added comically, though not finding anything funny about it.

Matt stopped and turned to her. An unidentifiable expression on his face. Maybe regret? After a short moment, he seemed to recover and answered, "Lucky for me, I got an exact replica."

CHAPTER 27

MATT

Matt sat out on the balcony sipping black coffee while Liz was in the shower. He wanted so badly to jump in there with her. The sweat beads that trickled down her neck during their run made it devastatingly hard to resist. But he had to. He needed to take a minute, disconnect and think.

It was getting out of hand. He knew it.

Why did it seem like every innocent question she asked, could lead to questions that were impossible to answer? He set his coffee mug down and rubbed his forehead. His heart started racing at the sudden fear of what he was going to do if she never recovered. He couldn't focus on never having Lizzy back. His mind wouldn't even enter that existence. He only allowed himself to focus on the pressure of having to live this lie. It overpowered him, making him lose all rational thought.

Annoyed by reminders from the doctor's voicemails to be honest with her to avoid negative setbacks.

He exhaled slowly, trying to regain control. But it was impossible. He couldn't get thoughts of her out his head. And they were random as hell. Flashes of his real wife mixed with the woman who didn't remember being her. Every smile, laugh, cry, plead. Every covered emotion when she'd considered telling him but decided it was better off to keep lying.

How is this different?

Dammit. He had to stop comparing the situation. It wasn't the same. It just wasn't. He was protecting her well-being. He wanted to call the good doctor and tell him the whole story. Then ask him what he would do if it were his wife. His love. His everything. He couldn't imagine how breaking the innocent woman's heart would fix everything.

Maybe those weren't the doctor's words exactly, but supposedly, it was a step in the right direction. No, he refused to believe it. He could do this without help.

Still, he couldn't shake the place in his heart, no matter how small it might have been, that connected with the Liz from three years ago. The woman who made a solid choice to keep a lie. How could he be sympathizing with the woman who lied and betrayed? It wasn't right. She was clearly putting a spell on him. Her new innocence was making him lose his mind.

They are not the same person.

He was on the verge of coming out of his skin when the balcony door opened. Her brilliant and familiar smile easing him almost instantly. She sat on the other side of the table, wearing denim shorts and a white blouse.

"You win," she smirked.

"I usually do. But how so this time?" It was as if the last few minutes in his mind never happened when she smiled at him.

"I don't run. I will leave you to your morning routine, and no longer interfere." She held her hands up as if to concede.

"That's too bad, I enjoyed having you with me," he admitted.

"You enjoyed making fun of me."

"All the same." His smirk faded after a moment. "By the way, I wanted to ask you if you'd like to go visit my parents beach house this weekend. They don't typically see us throughout the year except on holidays, so they want to squeeze as much out of our summer as they can." He wasn't sure who that excuse was for. Liz sure wouldn't need it. She'd been asking to "meet" his parents for weeks.

As expected, Liz beamed. "I would love that." For a moment, it looked like there was more she wanted to say, but then decided against it and leaned back in her chair.

Matt smiled and finished his coffee. "It will only be for an afternoon and then we'd leave after dinner." He was letting it be known that there was no way they'd be spending the night there again. And he'd tell his mother the same. The minimal amount of effort to appease her.

CHAPTER 28

LIZ

Francis and Robert Owen lived in a ranch-style beach house on Long Island. The interior wasn't spectacular, but it was cozy. What Liz loved most was the back porch, dark wood planks surrounded by a birchwood fence. A few short steps led straight to the beach, the last one buried in sand. Liz could have stayed out there for hours. But she and Francis only stayed long enough for her mother-in-law to show her the view and her plants.

Liz appreciated how hard the couple tried to make her feel safe and welcome. Francis had insisted it was exciting because she felt like she'd made a new friend and all her stories will be "brand-new". Mr. Owen Senior, at no surprise to Liz, talked about his boat, Sydney.

And then there were Ben and Megan, who mainly kept to themselves. Or rather, Megan on her phone for work-related reasons and Ben appearing utterly busy around the house. For someone who once insisted that they were pretty close, Ben hardly said three words to Liz since they got in that afternoon.

For the tenth time since she'd woken from the accident, Liz could feel something was being hidden from her. The more time she spent with Matt, the more she noticed subtle changes in his moods. There were times when he'd look at her as if she were truly his everything. It was undeniable how much he loved her. But her doubts, the few she still had, weren't unwarranted. They were valid. There were unmistakable glimpses of hurt and anger in Matt's eyes. Noticeable changes in his tone when she questioned or asked about something specific about their life together. She couldn't be sure. But in those brief flashes of fury in his eyes, she could swear she was being *accused* of something. She may have lost her memories, but she wasn't blind.

Maybe it was because he missed his wife. *His Lizzy.* Perhaps he was blaming her for keeping his wife away. Or maybe the other way around, and he's frustrated at *Lizzy* for refusing to "come back".

And she would come back.

Liz had accepted that she would live this life temporarily, until she got her memories back and then maybe things would make sense to her. Or she would just disappear into non-existence, where she felt like she'd come from.

"That's enough of the cucumbers dear, thank you." Francis broke into her thoughts. She hadn't realized she was still chopping away.

"Of course. Are they thick enough?"

"They're perfect," the woman answered with barely a glance at the sliced vegetable.

"I'm sorry, I was a little distracted, I guess." Liz wouldn't shy away from opening up to the only mother she'd known. And Francis seemed like the type of person to appreciate it.

"Oh I've been known to let my mind wander while I'm in the kitchen," Francis admitted and then gently lifted the knife through Liz's hand. "But it's always best not to when you're handling sharp objects."

"It's just strange being here and not remembering all of you, when you're all so...familiar."

"I understand." Her warm smile spread through Liz like something she'd never known. It was hearty, loving and everything that Liz hadn't realized she'd been missing.

"I wish I'd met you all sooner," Liz turned back to work on the salad.

"Well we've been insisting you come for weeks," she barked, throwing her hands up defensively. Then immediately patted Liz's back lightly and lowered her voice. "I was beginning to think the Fourth of July weekend was the last we'd see you." The woman complained, giving Liz a light shake, then something flashed in her eyes and she dashed to the oven.

Liz watched her mother in law for a moment, then turned back to the bowl, her eyes locked in a daze wondering why a spark went off in her chest at Francie's words. And maybe she wouldn't have thought twice about her comment if her pupils didn't double in size as soon as she'd spoken them. Liz tried to think back to everything Matt had told her about that weekend. All she could remember is that he'd told her it was uneventful. And that she'd gone out for a bit with Megan. Her eyes and mind were out of control. Suddenly, being in the kitchen made her feel claustrophobic. She needed to stop wondering about that mystery weekend and move on before someone thought she was having a stroke. She tossed some dill into the salad and took it to the dining table.

Everyone had assumed their seats except for her and Francis, who still had her head in the oven.

Matt held out a chair for her.

Liz quickly glanced around the table to see if the setting seemed familiar to her. If they sat around this same table as her husband had insisted they had. Thanksgiving, Christmas, random family celebrations and some weekends in the Summer.

Nothing. To her, it was all new.

What wasn't new, however, was the tension she once again felt between Matt and Ben. Something far too heavy to be an alleged object they fought about.

"Matt, didn't you say the wine is kept in the basement?" Liz asked, putting on her most innocent tone.

"Yeah, we put out a few bottles here, if—"

"Could you show me?" Liz lifted an eyebrow and offered a small smile.

"Uh—yeah sure." Matt stood and led them down to the wine cellar. The large room appeared clean in the dim lighting but smelled musty and was a tad colder than upstairs. The wine collection was anything but limited, stored in a wall to wall symmetrical wooden grid.

Matt traced one hand over a few of the flat laying bottles, while the other still held on to Liz's hand. He spun her around. "I know why we're really down here," he grinned, staring at her lips. He pulled her towards him and pressed his lips to hers.

She smiled underneath his lips and pulled away lightly.

"Okay, so I didn't ask you to show me down here for wine," Liz admitted.

"I know when you're lying," he said teasingly and pulling her back towards him.

With another light push, she held her hand on his chest and looked up at him. "And I know when you're lying."

He gave her a quizzical look.

"What you told me about what's going on between you and Ben is bullshit."

His eyes narrowed and she caught that same glimpse of anger before he glanced up the stairs. "What do you think you know?"

"I think I know that 'borrowing something without asking' is a load of crap for the way you keep looking at him."

Matt blinked. "Well it's true."

"Well did he give it back?" she shrugged to point out the simple solution.

"Drop it, Liz." His warning tone made her flinch. He took a breath and stepped away from her.

She watched him for a short moment. "It's not that simple, is it?" She raised an eyebrow.

He turned back to her. An unreadable expression, "No."

"Okay. I'll drop this," she agreed, and stalked past him up the stairs.

CHAPTER 29

MATT

Matt had a bad feeling about what Liz meant by dropping *this*. What was he doing wrong? All he wanted was to protect her. He only wished she trusted him. Most of the time, she did. Other times, she would gaze at him with doubting eyes. Either way, he needed to be more careful. He couldn't have Liz remembering all the wrong things. Not yet.

The doctors' voicemail kept playing back in his head as they sat down to join the rest of the family at the table. Keeping her away from all things that could trigger memories of her being with Ben was all he wanted to do. Including Ben himself.

"This all looks so good, Francis," Liz commented.

His mother raised both her eyebrows. "Let me know if you like it." They all knew Francis had made Liz's favorite dish without letting her know it. Eggplant rollatini wasn't something his mother made often, but when she did, it was typically at Liz's request. Matt looked at his mother thoughtfully. Apparently, she had decided to do a memory experiment of her own.

"This is delicious," Liz beamed. "Do you usually make vegetarian dishes?"

"No, we're all meat lovers here. But...once in a while..." Francis shrugged and dug into her own plate.

Ben and Megan were quietly sitting across from Matt and Liz, barely looking around the table, much less each other. He spotted Liz lifting her glass as if she was about to toast.

"Thank you so much for having me over," he heard her say. "I was beginning to think I wasn't welcome here, I mean after that fourth of July weekend."

The color drained out of Matt's face as his eyes shot to his wife. She bothered with nothing more than a simple innocent glance at him, but held an overly enthusiastic grin as she waited for an answer. She didn't seem to be addressing anyone particular at the table.

Ben coughed.

Megan set her fork down and put her hands on her lap.

But the one person who didn't seem surprised by Liz's sudden interest in the last time they were there—was his mother.

Matt tilted his head towards his wife. "Liz why would you want to talk about that weekend right now?"

"What's the matter? I'm simply stating the last time we were here and pointing out that no one had asked me to come visit since," she paused. "Why is that?"

Matt's eyes shot to his mother, who caught his glare and lifted an eyebrow in question. His mother was never the type to feel guilty about anything, especially when she was the one telling the truth.

He set down his glass and snuck a glance at his brother, who had his jaw clenched and staring at the rim of his own glass. Matt took a silent breath and let out a short laugh, "You're always welcome here, Liz." It was all he could think to say at that moment.

"Mmm-hmm, well I know that now." Liz smiled at her in-laws.

"Liz."

"Apparently, they've been trying to get us to visit for weeks now," she continued, beaming, yet her voice growing louder.

"He probably just forgot," his mother blurted. She didn't seem so sure of herself now. Confrontation was never something his mother could handle.

"I thought I was the one with the memory loss."

"I didn't forget anything, Liz," Matt announced angrily.

"Can you two please do this someplace else?" Rob barked.

"Fine." Matt stood abruptly.

"I meant another time, Matt, we're having dinner," his father softened.

Matt ignored his father and held out a hand to his wife. "Lizzy?"

She glanced at him. "You know I would, but I seem to get a lot more answers just from other people at this table," she grinned widely at the others seated. Then turned to him, her eyes cold. "I get nothing from you."

He felt the flames traveling up his neck before they flashed through his eyes. He was surely turning an angry color and was about to raise his voice until he caught a warning look from both his parents.

Breathing out slowly, he looked at his wife, thoughtfully. "Please."

Thankfully giving in to his pleading look, she rose from the table and followed as he led them into the first bedroom down the hall. Closing the door behind them, he spun her around to face him. "Look, I can see you're angry, but that wasn't necessary. there's a— "

"What? A perfectly good reason for keeping me from your family, the only family I really have?" she insisted.

"Telling them that I wasn't ready? Why, why would you do that?"

"I know it doesn't make sense to you, but Liz, I'm just— I'm following doctors' orders, you need to trust me."

"What doctor's orders?"

"That your memories need to come back in a certain order."

"But he said they would naturally, Matt. You're keeping things from me. No, you're keeping *something* from me," she insisted, pointing a finger at him. "Is it something that happened that weekend?"

The look on her face suggested she wasn't letting this go. She was growing tired, he could see it in her eyes every time he slipped and would reveal any type of resentment toward her. He couldn't help it. It was all too fresh.

He'd noticed a pattern, too. Every time he would try to remind her about their love and their history, he'd fall into the moment alongside her. And then remember that moments before her accident...he'd decided to let it all go.

To forget it, forget her.

Ironically, she'd been the one to forget it all.

And it hurt. Even at no fault or control of her own, she'd forgotten all the amazing memories and years together. The only one he'd wished she'd permanently forget was when he left her to go to Ireland. When he told her he needed space. For years, he'd considered it to be the biggest mistake of his life. He never imagined how big a mistake it was, until a few weeks ago.

"Honey, if there was something you absolutely needed to know, I would tell you."

She looked at him and frowned, as if that wasn't a good enough answer. She ran her fingers through her hair and turned away from him, clearly frustrated. With her face in her hands, she quietly paced a small distance before lifting her head. Her exasperated expression slowly fading, she intently scanned the dimly lit room's surroundings, with extreme interest.

"I've been in this room before," she muttered.

Matt's head shot up.

"Recently," she continued, almost in a whisper.

Matt glanced around and wanted to slap himself. What was he thinking? His head screamed to get her out of there—as quickly as possible. But he was frozen in place.

Liz took small steps, her eyes focusing on random objects in the spacious room, then the window and then finally settling on the chair.

The chair.

The damned chair where she sat and cried while he told her he couldn't forgive her. Where her life was falling apart.

Something between sadness, fear and scrutiny was in her dark eyes as she stared at that chair. Goosebumps shot up her arms and she hugged herself. Every ounce of him wanted to reach out, pull her into his arms and tear her away from one of her darkest moments.

But he couldn't.

He should embrace his instinct to protect her. Protect her from any unforgiving memories scraping their way to the surface. Instead, he stood there, unable to fight the burning need for her to remember that night.

To find out if she would fight for him.

Snapping out of his thoughts, he paced to her side and lifted her chin. He stared deep into her confused eyes. They burned into his before pulling back as if to see him from a distance.

"I was here with you," she recalled.

"Of course you were, this is where we usually stay when— "

"No," her voice louder and angrier. "No, no," she blinked away. "I was upset. I was very, very upset." Her voice grew louder in a panic.

He instantly grabbed her shoulders, ready to shake her out of her cold memory. But he just held them, as she looked up at him with desperate eyes.

"Why was I so upset?" she whispered.

"Lizzy, why don't you come back outside, we can—"

She sprung loose from his hold. "Why was I so upset, were we fighting?" Her eyes flashed down and to her left. "No...no we weren't fighting. We were—no you were calm." She threw her hands in the air and shut her eyes. "God dammit, why can't I hear anything you're saying? Why?" She grabbed his arms and shook him, her eyes were pleading, but in a convicting way.

His heart was being attacked by a massive shredder and everything seemed to move in slow motion. Everything around him a blur. She was breaking down in front of him and he couldn't do anything to stop it. He wanted more than anything to turn back time, so that he could have taken her into another room, or turn back to tell Megan there was no way in hell he'd bring Liz for a visit. Hell, he'd even turn it as far back as before her accident and have a do-over on that night if it meant she wouldn't have to be living this terrifying moment.

"I think this is normal, Liz. In—in fact, I'm sure it is." He shut his eyes and rubbed the top of his lids, knowing he was going to regret taking the doctor's advice. "What else are you feeling?"

She turned away. "Nothing," her shoulders slacked in defeat.

"Look, why don't I call the doctor and let him know you're having—."

"Let him know the first memory I have of my husband is in this dark, creepy room and he's saying things that are upsetting me?"

"It wasn't like that, Liz," he whispered.

She swallowed hard and tears started rolling down her cheeks. "No," she said softly and shook her head. "My only memory of the one person I've doubted since the day I met him...doesn't surprise me at all."

That hurt him more than if she had re-told the story of how she ended up with his brother. He took a deep breath, reminding himself that the woman before him needed help, not resentment. "Honey, it was a small, stupid fight, it happened just before your accident, you don't even know what we were talking about." And he hoped it stayed that way.

At least for now.

She turned her head slowly and walked back to the chair, gazing at it, as if waiting for it to reveal something else to her. "I may not know what you're saying to me, but I know you're hurting me," she murmured.

He came up behind her. He wouldn't touch her yet, he just stood for a minute.

"Please leave me alone." Her eyes were closed, and her voice was exhausted.

"I'm not leaving you alone here."

Hesitating for a moment, he turned her around. Then pulled her onto the edge of the bed. Kneeling before her, he took both her hands in his. She wasn't letting this go, and if re-assurance is what she needed, then he was going to give it to her. He was going to save her *his* way.

"Okay," he whispered, with an exhausted breath. "The last time we were in this room, it wasn't pleasant. We, uh, we had a bad night."

She looked back at him. "You said it was small and stupid."

"So you were listening."

She eyed him skeptically, "Who started it?"

"Ha, probably you. Don't remember, we didn't have a chance to lay the blame afterwards."

"What was it about?"

This was leading to more lies. Looking at her now, with her desperate expression, he knew there was nothing he could come up with to alleviate her doubts. Or justify the coldness she felt in this room.

No. Lying wouldn't help.

He stood and knew his expression had turned a tad colder when she looked up at him. He took her hand and pulled her to stand on her feet. It was time he took back control of his marriage. "That's not how this is going to work, Lizzy." his tone more definite, insistent. "I'm not a stranger, I'm certainly not your enemy no matter what that fight was about. I'm your husband, your best friend. And you need to start trusting me."

She stared at him, her expression unreadable. But if he were to guess, she wanted to hear more of what he had to say.

"I might have lied about some things, but only because I only want you to remember the best times. No matter what greater power is putting you through right now, I'm sure the intention isn't to make you relive the harsh ones. All you need to know is I love you—truly and unconditionally."

It wasn't until that moment, as he was proclaiming his unconditional love to her that he realized how much he truly missed Liz. He wished to God she could hear him right now.

The real Liz.

Liz arched an eyebrow, not tense, in the slightest. In fact, she watched him with the most amused yet grateful eyes. "That's about as honest as I could ask. I guess you're right. I guess I don't need to know more. Not unless it matters, anyway," she added.

"To further my...honesty, I guess I was still a little mad about our fight for the few days you were back home from the hospital."

She seemed taken aback by that.

"Which is crazy and selfish, I know. But I don't care anymore." He came closer to meaning it than he ever imagined possible.

He surveyed the room once more, still holding her hand. "There's nothing here for you." He focused on her, urging her to do the same. "But there's plenty for us at home," he winked.

Then she did the last thing he'd expected. She threw her arms around him and buried her face in his neck. The way Lizzy used to. He smiled to himself, knowing he'd made the right choice in healing her with his love. Not making her face her fears.

"I'm sorry I've been difficult. And for over-reacting in front of your family." She half covered her face.

He shrugged. "It's not like I just brought you to meet my parents for the first time," he lifted her palm and kissed it. "You ready to go back out?"

He recognized the hesitant expression now on his wife's face, her lower lip being pulled on one side. There was something she needed to say. He smiled to himself at the fact that some things didn't leave her.

She released her lip and shook her head. "Only to say goodbye," she replied, her eyes turning suggestive. "Take me home."

CHAPTER 30

LIZ

Matt made her request the simplest thing in the world.
He took her hand and led her out to the now separated
family members. Francis and Megan clearing the table, Rob
reading in the den and Ben having a cigarette on the back
porch. They said their goodbyes to the women and Matt's
father, but somehow Liz knew better than to suggest they do
the same with Ben. Francis graciously accepted their early
departure and relentlessly insisted they take leftovers, since
"Lizzy barely touched her favorite dish."

A short hour later, they arrived at their home. The place
suddenly feeling more like it to her. It may have been
aggressive, back in the guest room of his parent's beach
house, but it was honest. And that's all she had wanted. The
man cared deeply for her, of that there was no doubt. Since
waking up, cold, lost and disoriented as strangers
surrounded her, he'd been the one person protecting her.
The anger she'd often see in his eyes didn't bother her as
much as one would imagine. It was a strong feeling, and
she preferred it over emptiness. Somehow, Liz never felt
empty. She knew there were emotions within her—the real
her—that were far away. She could feel she was an expressive
person. Nothing like Megan. Since Megan was the only other
younger woman Liz knew, she compared herself to her quite
often.

"Sure you're not hungry?" Matt called from the kitchen.

It was still early. The digital clock displayed just before nine and it had been a long day.

"I'm alright."

He emerged from the kitchen holding two glasses of red wine which seemed to have already eased her. She smiled up at him. "Thank you."

Matt motioned for her to sit with him on their sofa. She sat beside him and felt the most ease. She automatically placed her head on his shoulder. Though they'd been intimate before, she hadn't completely trusted him until tonight. She'd caught him in a lie about their past and he didn't even flinch. It was as though he didn't regret whatever it took to protect her. Was it right to fall for him? Though the good doctor explained to her how memory recovery worked, she couldn't help the sinking feeling that she'd lose him when her memory returned. She would disappear and the old Liz would reclaim her husband.

It was silly to think of it that way, but it was nonetheless how she felt. Her inevitable disappearance was very real to her.

Things will start coming back to her soon. She knew it. And she feared it.

"What are you thinking about?" he murmured, his lips touching the top of her head.

"How I wish I could stay here forever." The strangely painful honesty.

He pulled his head up and seemed to go somewhere for a moment. She looked up at him and found his eyes focused on the carpet. A memory? "Maybe I should ask what you're thinking about."

He looked back at her, undeniable guilt on his face.

"Liz, I know you think that I don't understand what you went through those first few days after you woke up.

And maybe I can't fully, but I know it was unimaginably difficult. Frightening. If I didn't say it enough, I'll make up for it now, I am sorry. I feel like I failed you. As a husband. As your partner," his voice faded. "You wouldn't have even been in that—" he took a swig of his wine and placed it on the table, swallowing hard and then turned to face her. "I promise you will never feel alone again." His words seemed to have a deeper meaning for him than her.

She couldn't control the need for him any longer. She'd held back long enough. Ever since that night they shared, his advances had been subtle and teasing. She wouldn't hold back anymore. If she was going to lose him as she knew him right then, she needed to take advantage now.

She set her glass down and turned back, pushing herself further into him. Placing her hands on his chest, she leaned in for a long kiss that she wanted to savor. Pushing aside her fear of losing him, she broke away and looked up at him. "It's been a long day. I think I'm going to shower and go to bed." She smiled to herself and turned to walk up the stairs, leaving him alone in the living room. Her not so subtle way of giving him a taste of his own medicine.

Their master bathroom was heaven. And though her escape had different intentions, a shower did sound pleasantly needed. The pearl white tiles dulled as the steam spread through the spacious room. The mirror fogged just before she stepped behind the wide glass frame onto the ridged porcelain surface. The hot water barely scorched her skin.

Yes, this was what she needed.

It was, after all, a long emotional day and perhaps Matt would leave her to end her evening in solidarity, but somehow, the longing in his eyes just before she turned away, made her doubt it was the last she'd see of him that night. Surely, he'd be back, when she was through, emerging out into the cool bedroom in her bathrobe. The same one he'd once painfully placed around her shoulders when she'd pursued him.

Perhaps she'd play the same game.

Or perhaps she shouldn't. Time was not her friend. Not with the fleeting memories she'd been having. Though unclear, the visions of the past were still flashing into her mind.

Submerging her hair into her personal waterfall, she closed her eyes. The pressure against the back of her neck somehow releasing an incredible amount of stress. With the now perfectly warm water filling her ears, she opened her eyes and mouth to fill the rest of her senses.

A dark figure behind the steamed glass appeared. He warned her with a tap on the glass before stepping in. The same desire was in his eyes, only now with a hint of humor behind them.

He crossed the short distance to her, placing his warm hands on her waist, he pushed her lightly against the wall.

"Your game won't work on me," he insisted.

"Don't be so sure of that."

"Maybe I let you win," he murmured before crushing his lips over hers. He pushed her wet hair behind her and traced his fingers down her neck, between her breasts and then down to her navel. He paused to tickle her there, making her squirm into him and before she realized it, his hand reached her pelvic bone, making her jump slightly.

It wasn't enough. She needed more of him. She was desperate for more. She began to slide down when he pulled her back up and pinned her back to the wall.

He gave her a tempered smile before sliding himself down her torso, slowly licking her. His lips and tongue teased her relentlessly, until his tongue finally delved deeper. Her hands reached out but found nothing to grab as she melted. They landed back on the top of his head. Her fingers digging into his skull. How was it even possible to feel this good? She cried out and started to shake, which only made him move faster and stronger, until she climaxed and melted into his arms.

He stood, turning the knob to shut off the water. Her eyes flew open. He was barely wet, and she hadn't had the chance to use soap before he started drying her off. He wrapped the towel around her and carried her back into their bedroom. She glanced at the bed that he'd already turned down for them. Their unfinished wine glasses sat on the night table. And the main lights were turned down, leaving only the dimmed pin-up wall lamps on either side of the bed.

He pulled the towel over her shoulders and shuffled her wet hair. She laughed and fell into him, losing her balance. He chuckled along with her and pulled her onto the bed.

"I wasn't done with my shower."

"And you won't be getting much sleep either."

"You're going to be very disappointed in about twenty minutes," she joked.

He seemed lost in her laugh for a moment before kissing and guiding her farther onto the bed. She slid a hand onto his bare chest and one over his back, pulling him closer. She felt him harden instantly as he glided over her. His body was smooth, or maybe it was his touch that was so gentle. He didn't take the time to take her in the way she had him. But then, a married couple who know each other well unclothed, might rarely do that anymore.

"You are beautiful," he reassured, leaning back just enough to look into her eyes when he said it.

"Stop stalling." She pulled him back down to her.

He kissed her chest, then her stomach, continuing to tease her as if they had all the time in the world to be with each other. She closed her eyes at that thought. Her heart ached again, but only for a fleeting second before Matt wrapped a hand around the back of her neck.

"What is it?" his eyes sensual yet concerned.

I'm going to miss you when she comes back.

She shook her head and gave a small smile. Her thoughts wouldn't make any sense to anyone but her. And there was no point in sharing. She knew he wasn't convinced.

After a brief moment of searching her eyes, he kissed her forehead lightly. "You'd tell me?"

Liz only nodded and let out a breath, releasing the negative energy that crept into her mind during such a wonderful moment. "I want all of you."

He grinned and slid his hands down her skin around her lower back, then lifting her into him. She was wet and waiting. Her back arched towards him just before he pushed inside her, releasing a moan from her throat. Her head sinked deeper into the pillow with every thrust. She enjoyed every inch of him touching her. Savored it. She didn't let her mind wander to the *when again's* and *what if next times.* Liz let herself stay in the moment. Embracing the thickness of him inside her, loving the way his lower torso rubbed against hers. He sped up his rhythm, vigorously sending her into another intense rapture bursting within her.

CHAPTER 31

MATT

Matt watched her breathing slow to a steady, silent pace and knew she was asleep, her head still tucked under his shoulder. It wasn't likely that he'd fall into a peaceful slumber beside her that night. His heart still raced with excitement and now guilt. He wanted her. Too much. He needed her. He needed her without the question of what this meant; forgiveness or empty desire.

He turned away from the woman—the stranger lying next to him. He missed Lizzy more than he ever imagined. If only for a moment, she could come back to him. Wake up remembering everything and still find herself in the comfort and safety of his arms.

Would that be enough for her to trust that it was okay to come back? That he won't hurt or abandon her. Never again. If this cruel disease of the human mind would just give him one minute with her. Sixty seconds would surely be enough time to prove to her that it was safe.

He would hold her close and tell her that nothing else mattered. That their world she thought was falling apart was only going through a small test. He'd tell her that as long as they were together, they'd overcome anything.

Nothing mattered.

But didn't it? How long would that moment last before his anger started rushing back like an aftershock, and he'd be back to the rage and resentment that pushed her right into those headlights. Throwing harsh words that he'd never imagined at the woman he trusted more than anyone.

So far, her memory loss, the fact that she'd been as innocent as the first day they met, had been the reason he'd been able to stay so collected. That he'd been able to love her and hold her without the stinging awareness of her betrayal.

She was without a doubt, innocent, and therefore not Liz. Liz wasn't innocent. She deceived him.

With the doubt now fresh in his mind, his arm jerked from underneath her.

Get it together.

He saw her shift and frown. Then her eyes opened.

Dammit.

"I'm sorry," she propped herself up a little, "I must have been suffocating you."

"No, you could never." He looked down at her from his upright position and forced a smile. "I just needed to sit up for a minute. That's all." He bent down and kissed the top of her head. "I'm sorry I woke you."

She didn't seem to believe him. There was either uncertainty in her eyes or hesitation. As if she wanted to ask something, but decided against it.

She reluctantly laid back down. "You don't have to be sorry," she yawned, "I do."

"What?"

She was half asleep at this point. "I've been difficult, and you've been patient. Not pushing me. You're just letting me be me." She smiled softly; her eyes closed. "I don't know what the doctor ordered but I know I'm in good hands."

...The downfall of not doing so could be very dangerous and lead to serious mental setbacks if her memories start flooding back negatively before she's ready.

The end of Dr. Tai's voicemail replayed in Matt's head. "I'd never do anything to hurt you, Lizzy," he promised. Hoping it went further than her ears. He needed his wife to hear them too.

* * *

At 7:00 am the next morning—Sunday morning—Matt found himself staring out the window in their kitchen. Fresh, hot coffee pouring down his throat. It was something he'd find Lizzy doing on weekends when she couldn't sleep in.

Perhaps sleeping wasn't his problem. Perhaps it was who he was sleeping with. And how unfair it was. Truthfully, it was unfair to all three of them.

To his missing wife, his Lizzy, who was being kept away somewhere until he did all the right things, in the right order and at the right pace to bring her back. Exactly how the doctor ordered.

It was unfair to the woman Liz sent in her place, who lay upstairs in their bed at that very moment, innocent to the deception. Confused with his mixed emotions of care, love and resentment. He should have been fair to her from the start. And what happened a few short hours ago was a mistake.

But mostly—at least at the very moment—unfair to him. How could life throw him this cruel curve and then not even give him a day to deal with it? Why did he have to be forced to put his anger and hurt aside? It was too soon to test his love. And downright unfair.

The doorbell rang, interrupting his thoughts. Matt frowned, glancing up at the time display on the oven. He pulled open the door to find Ben on the other side of the frame. His look was tentative and unapproving. Matt glared at him, waiting.

"Is Liz around?"

"She's asleep," Matt said flatly.

Ben glanced inside and quickly licked his lips. "Can we talk?"

Matt sighed. He knew this wasn't good, but something told him his brother wasn't going away. Matt glanced upstairs before stepping out of the apartment and closing the front door behind him. He stood there—arms crossed, waiting.

"You can't go on like this," Ben breathed.

Matt glared at his brother. Not bothering to ask why he thought *this* had anything to do with him. Or why he of all people thought he was in any place to give advice. He was just as much to blame for Liz's situation as Matt was. Matt threw his arms in the air and tried to keep his voice down. "What am I supposed to do? Tell her what happened between the two of you and that I'd just found out about it? That I decided I couldn't live with it, so she's on her own?"

"No, of course not. But you can't lead her on either," Ben insisted.

"Stay out of it," Matt hissed.

"And you're not doing much to make her remember," Ben went on, ignoring Matt's threat. "That hypnosis stunt was..." he paused, looking up at Matt. "You're not sleeping with her, are you?

Matt glanced away.

"Matt!"

But before Matt had a chance to shoot him another warning look, Ben held up his hands. "Look, I'm not going to tell you that you should wait until you resolve your issues, but if you still plan on giving up on your marriage then you can't do that." Ben flashed a disgusted look. "It's just wrong."

"Don't talk to me about morals."

"I'm not saying that what we did was okay, and keeping it from you was unjustifiable, but what's going to happen when she gets her memory back, and asks you what that all meant?"

Matt was getting frustrated and angrier by the second. But he couldn't risk Liz overhearing. Frustration building and annoyance at his brothers' sense.

"You do realize this is the same woman, right? Liz isn't just going to come back to us and forget the last few weeks," Ben pointed out.

Matt stayed silent. He should throw him out, punch him, anything—but a part of him locked in the burning outrage because he knew, bone deep, he needed to hear this. He knew it, but he wasn't ready. He wasn't ready to follow doctors' orders; taking her to familiar places, under no pressure, talking with her, answering her questions, showing her objects of meaning. Everything she'd been begging him for, but he selfishly avoided.

Telling her that she picked out the right mug would help too. When you tell them that they are headed in the right direction, it builds confidence and open mindedness. It triggers a possibility for them, instead of fear of never recalling a single memory. If only to himself, he'd admit it.

He wasn't ready to face Lizzy.

"Get out."

Ben sighed. "Fine. But she's going to get her memory back. And when she finds out that you've been holding her back because of selfish reasons, this decision you made to end your marriage might no longer be yours to make."

CHAPTER 32

LIZ

The car door opened for Liz as soon as they pulled up to the circular driveway of the venue. Her long black dress fit well with the formally attired crowd by the main entrance. Liz eyed and admired the lavish entrance. She wondered if they came to these types of events often.

Matt appeared at her side before her foot hit the ground and held out his forearm, giving her his half grin that calmed her nerves, and was no doubt part of his charm when they met. She took his arm and let him lead her toward the open mahogany doors. Her husband leaned into her subtly.

"Don't worry, we don't do these types of things often, this is more of an annual event."

"I'm glad Megan helped me pick out a dress."

"I'm glad that everything in your closet is new to you, or you would have insisted on going shopping for this."

Something about his reference to the event, *for this*, seemed resentful.

"You don't sound like you want to be here."

He glanced at her and lifted an eyebrow. "You're very perceptive," he paused. "I'm just very protective, I suppose. I don't like you to be around people you don't know...or trust."

She smiled, relieved that he hadn't tried to lie again when she called him out on his feelings. She tugged his arm close. "I'm not only perceptive with you, you know." She raised an eyebrow at him and turned to the crowd. "I like to think I could peg the ones I can trust." She glanced at him and shrugged. "Besides, I have a game I'd like to try."

"It wouldn't be out of character for you."

Liz frowned at the comment.

What she knew of the event was that it was political. Less than a gala, but more than just a party. Supporting the local district's politicians was apparently something his parents were religious about. And therefore, Matt and Ben had to participate. Matt had said the plates cost a good portion of his last paycheck.

Liz continued her analysis. If they were here for the district where Matt and Ben had gone to school, there would be mutual friends here. Possibly friends they only connected with on such occasions. Therefore, not close friendships, but not entirely lost. Just as she was about to proudly state her assessment to her husband, a tall dark-haired woman, who appeared to be in her early thirties, raced over to them.

"Lizzy! You're alive," she exclaimed.

"Oh boy," Matt murmured.

"I got this," Liz muttered through her teeth.

Matt looked at her surprised. "What?"

"What's her name?"

"Angel."

"An— Really?" She glanced up at him then shrugged as the woman finally reached them.

"Angel! Where've you been?" Liz exclaimed.

"Me? I've been calling you for weeks. Someone told me you hit your head in an accident?" The woman was exactly as she'd expected, upfront and vocal.

"No permanent damage." It wasn't entirely a lie. Liz believed her memories would be coming back. "I've been swamped with...lesson plans for the coming year. And we're renovating the kitchen, so of course I could never hear or find my phone. Anyway, how've you been? I *know* you have news." Liz insisted.

Somehow the woman appeared to be the type of person that typically talked about herself and always had "news" or gossip of some kind. Maybe it was Liz's strange sense of telling a personality or just her memory giving her an ounce.

"You know I do." Angel went on a brief summary of a guy named Frank from the office and how she was getting closer to getting to know him better. Although Angel's words faded to mumbling in the background as Liz glanced at Matt's amused face. Somehow, it didn't sound like Angel was close to anything with regard to this *Frank*.

"I'm coming over for wine next week, we'll catch up," Liz offered, before pulling Matt in the other direction with her.

"I'll come to you—want to see that new kitchen," Angel called.

"So, you want to get our kitchen redone huh?" Matt concluded after they were a safe distance away.

"What? No, that was just a—"

Matt shook his head, pointing a finger at her. "No, no, that didn't come from nowhere. Why would that be the first thing you thought of?"

Liz shrugged. "Maybe we could look into refreshing it a bit."

"Well we have to now!" He nodded his head back towards where Angel now stood, talking an earful to someone else.

A short gentleman dressed in a sharp black suit with a white shirt and black bowtie, approached them holding a tray of tall champagne-filled flutes. Matt let go of Liz's arm for a moment to grab two glasses and nod at the server.

Matt handed Liz her glass. He was about to say something when an older gentleman approached them. The unfamiliar man wore a gray, well-tailored suit, a remarkable watch, and shiny cufflinks. Liz suspected him to be one of the honored guests or host.

"Counselman O'Reilly," Matt acknowledged.

"Matthew," the man acknowledged with a nod. "Liz, how are you? Great to see you both again. I just saw your parents, Matt. Always a pleasure."

Matt nodded. Clearly not a mutual feeling. Matt didn't seem to be a pretender. Liz could be it for him.

She reached her hand to touch the Counselman. "Equally a pleasure, Counselman. These events really do get better every year." She gave her warmest smile.

The white-haired man appeared very pleased with the compliment. "Thank you, thank you." He looked around, admiring the crowd and decoration. "We do try to keep it up to scale." He seemed to have spotted other guests nearby. "Thanks again for your support," he patted Matt on the arm before disappearing.

Matt leaned in and mumbled into the top of her head. "You are good at this. If you keep it up, I might put you to the test with a difficult crowd."

"I'm game, but you wouldn't," she challenged.

"You know me too well."

CHAPTER 33

MATT

It was as though she'd never left. Her grace, her attention; she was ready for anything, for anyone. She was doing more than just covering the effects of her injury. She was charming the crowd and enjoying herself. Enjoying being free of the looks of concern, and people tip toeing around her. He hadn't been blind to how much that annoyed her, but now saw how much she yearned to be *normal*.

Whatever that meant to her.

Liz seemed to feed off him pretty well when it came to how much a particular person or couple were liked by them.

The Millers for example, weren't their favorite couple. The few dinners and encounters with them in the past had been unbearable. The couple praised each other more in one night than you'd hear at the Academy Awards.

And Matt particularly approved of Liz's aversion of the "children" question from the Wyatt's. She touched Erica Wyatt's arm and insisted, "You will be the first to know! But tell me about yours." Sure, it wasn't difficult to assess that those asking about your plans for kids, already have their own, but to cleverly phrase the question without implying they have multiple—was genius.

He swapped out her near-empty glass for a full one and smiled at her. "You need a break."

She relaxed her shoulders, "Ugh, you're right. Do we sit yet?"

"No, let's get some air," Matt led her past the crowd of guests toward the back terrace of the venue. He couldn't have anymore "friends" popping up before they could be seated. And Liz needed a break from all the smiling, small chatter, and faking. But more than that, he was worried about her overexerting her brain, if that was even a thing. Perhaps he'd know, if he bothered to call Dr. Tai back. Still, some fresh air, a quiet moment for just the two of them, and having her all to himself for a moment, sounded phenomenal.

Ben appeared before them, just as they got to the double doors of the back terrace. "Hey guys, how's it going? Liz, you alright?"

Matt mentally shook his head at the nerve of his brother being so casual with them. He wasn't letting it go. Ben was always overprotective of his sister-in-law, which Matt always appreciated, but now that he'd been caught up on their lie, he was just offended by it.

"Hey Ben," she glanced cautiously at Matt. "I'm great, Matt and I were just taking a break from the crowded room."

"Yeah, no, I noticed you've been making some rounds." He glared at Matt, "you sure that's a good idea?"

"You heard her; she's having a great time."

Ben didn't alter, he glared at Matt. "You don't think this is a little too much for her right now?"

Liz opened her mouth to speak but Matt couldn't help himself, "I would know if something was too much for her to handle; clearly, I have more faith in her than you do."

Liz put a hand on Matt's chest instead of questioning the aggression. Another sign that she trusted him. She turned to Ben and was about to say something but was interrupted by someone from a few feet away.

"What do we have here," called a voice Matt unfortunately recognized. "It's the Owen brothers wrapped up in a not so discrete heated discussion." Clyde O'Reilly approached them with a devilish smile.

"Here to support my father for another term," he said matter-of-factly, "very appreciated, of course." He turned to Liz. "Lizzy, always good to see you. You don't look like you were in any accident." His head-to-toe observation of Matt's wife was irritating him to no end. The bastard had some nerve.

Liz just held the man's stare, unamused. "I recover quickly."

"So little, yet so strong. Good for you Matt, well done."

Matt felt Ben's hand on his shoulder—Ben knew Matt was about to lose his cool and wanted him to think better of it.

Clyde was in every sense of the word, a dick. One might expect the guy to use his family name and money to get ahead and go into politics himself, even. But no, the guy married some arm candy idiot, and spent his days making problems for people in town. Starting with his job at the Board of Ed years ago, when he'd initiated a "cleaning house" on his second year, causing a major uproar with the PTA and school officials. He was removed from office shortly after and had since then become the sleazebag of the town.

Saying the Owens disrespected the guy, would be an understatement. They hated the guy.

"Hey Clyde. And where's your better half?" Matt muttered.

"That she is," Clyde agreed. "She couldn't make it today, unfortunately. Conflicting event."

Megan appeared from nowhere. "Liz, hey, why don't we go have a drink with Angel and... the others."

Liz shot Matt a confused look and let Megan drag her away. Matt sneered at Clyde who watched the woman disappear into the crowd.

"Nice seeing you again Clyde," Ben said through gritted teeth.

"I appreciate the lie. See you kids around." One thing Matt respected about Clyde—emphasis on *one*—was that the guy called out bullshit when he heard it. Not that Matt cared.

"Hopefully not too soon," Ben muttered before he turned to Matt. "Can I talk to you outside?"

"Why?"

"It's about Liz."

"Is that why Megan dragged her away?"

Ben held his hands up. "I'm not picking a fight with you. I just want to help."

Matt swallowed, glanced over at a distracted Liz with Megan, and walked out to the terrace. He stormed to the far end and held the rail, facing the pier, away from the accusing stare from his betraying brother.

"What are you doing?" Ben finally asked.

Matt breathed deep and turned to stare back at his brother with no intention of responding.

"Just tell her the truth. You two are better than this."

"Don't lecture me about my marriage."

"You can get through it."

"What do you suppose I do? I just tell her what happened? That'll confuse the hell out her and set her so far I won't be able to bring her back."

"Or you make her face the reason she's hiding," Ben snapped.

"You really are a cruel human being."

"I know it sounds awful, but I think the mind is a powerful thing and she needs to face this."

With all his force and anger, Matt pressed both hands on his brother's chest and pushed him. "It's your fault she's in this. You screwed with her mind. You took advantage of her when she was hurting and now she's too afraid to face... her life," he paused. He turned away from Ben and focused on a blurry cluster of lights on a yacht floating a good mile from the pier.

Any other day, Ben would have fought back. But not this time. This time he stood silently behind him. Matt could hear his breathing. He could hear his brother's mind going over what to say next. What he didn't understand was that this wasn't his to fix.

"She's afraid of losing you," Ben finally said in nearly a whisper. "She doesn't want a life without you."

"You think you know her so well."

"You know her better. You know why this is happening, the doctor told you this, didn't he? He's been asking you about her life. If anything traumatic happened recently that may be the cause of her memory loss?"

Matt turned and stared at him in shock.

"I've been reading," Ben cocked his head and glanced away.

"Why are you so interested?"

"Someone needs to figure out how to help her, Matt. I'm not going to let your jealousy and anger ruin both your lives."

Matt's temper boiled, and he gripped Ben's shirt.

"She's like a sister to me, Matt. She was never anything more," he paused and locked eyes with Matt. "What happened three years ago was a mistake we've both been regretting; I can promise you that."

Matt let his brother go in a forceful push and turned to head back to find Liz. His heart sank when he saw who was standing at the doorway.

Clyde stood peering at them, partially concealed by the shadow of the doorframe. The snide expression that would send chills through Matt if he weren't so heated at the moment.

"Sorry to interrupt," Clyde offered. "Thought you boys could use a beer to cool off out here," his lips stretching on one end before he held up his hands with a bottle of beer in one and two of the same in the other.

Matt forced himself to relax his shoulders in an effort to disguise the tension built up in him the moment he noticed the devious man. He wouldn't ask how much he'd heard. He wouldn't give him the satisfaction. Matt glanced down at the beers. "I'll take one," he offered, ignoring Ben's sneer.

Clyde handed Matt a bottle, who nearly winced at the temperature. Not because it was cold. But because it wasn't cold enough. This wasn't a bottle pulled out of a cooler in the last five minutes.

"On second thought. I'm good. I'll see you around Clyde." Matt stalked out of the room to search for his wife and call it a night.

CHAPTER 34

LIZ

Liz stretched out her arms in acceptance of the morning sun shining through their bedroom window. She shivered a little and went to turn down the air conditioning. She followed with turning the knob of the large window, letting it unfold until it was a nearly perfect ninety-degree angle. She heard her husband shift his weight and felt his admiring eyes on her.

"That's cruel," he murmured.

"Well, maybe I would have slept in longer if we stayed at the party last night."

"What's the point? We had dinner, a few drinks. What did you want to stay for, the speeches? It's the same one every year. I could recite it to you, if you'd like."

"No, thank you." She blinked and then turned to face him. "I'd prefer you telling me the truth."

He fell back in bed, dramatically. "Okay, it was me. Goodnight."

She bounced next to him on the bed, barely causing him to move. "Tell me about Clyde."

Matt stayed silent under the covers for a moment, long enough for her to wonder if he'd truly fallen asleep. Until he pulled down the cover and looked thoughtfully and, dare she think, cautiously into her eyes. "Why do you want to know about him?"

"Who is he? Why don't you and your brother like him? Did he do anything to you?"

"No, he didn't do anything," he paused. "He's just a... he's a long-time family...friend. He can be a dick sometimes, but he's nothing to worry about."

She waited for more, but there didn't seem to be any. She decided to accept his lacking response and offered a small smile. "What are you doing today?"

"I'm going to go talk to Dr. Tai. Would you like to come?"

"Don't I have to?"

"Not necessarily. The doctor did want to speak with me alone at some point about your progress. He suggested it would be less pressure to be honest if you weren't in the room."

"I could see that," she smirked.

"No one is going to kick you out of the room, but we just want to discuss ways to...bring you back."

Her heart sank. *You mean bring her back.*

"You alright?" Matt's eyebrows furred.

"Of course. Getting my memory back is...what I want."

"What you need," he corrected almost in a question.

Suddenly Matt didn't seem sleepy anymore, but concerned. He gave her a long, tender look before lifting himself off the bed. With nothing but his briefs on, he sat on the edge, holding her waist. His eyes searching hers as if looking for the truth behind them.

"Liz, you were practically begging me every day to take you back to the hospital. To get more evaluations done, try new things," he reminded. "You're hesitant now," he accurately observed. "What are you afraid of?"

She bit the side of her lip as her eyes wandered around the room. "I guess I just don't want you to be disappointed... if you're stuck with me."

His brows furrowed. He stilled while he glared at her. As if she were a hologram that he could see right through. She immediately regretted uttering the words and refused to breathe again until he spoke. She wasn't lying, part of her did wonder if he'd be disappointed if her memories never fully returned. She feared her memories more than she feared losing Matt. She knew it didn't make sense; she'd still have him, but there was an undeniable gut feeling that pained her every time she thought of getting her memory back. She feared the truths, the lies, and the reality. It was as if a death to the life she knew and loved awaited her. Visible chills ran up her arms and she clutched them.

Matt glanced down at them and then back into her eyes. "Liz?"

He always called her Lizzy.

"What if there is something I don't want to remember?"

He stared at her for a moment before answering. "Then we'll face it together."

There was something. "Is it bad?" the lump thickening in her throat.

He breathed out from his nose, swallowed and stepped close to kiss her on the forehead.

"You're going to be fine." He turned away from her abruptly and went to put his clothes on with sudden urgency.

She nodded nervously. "I want to get my memory back. I want to be the wife and woman you remember. I want our life back," she added, desperate for another reaction. She didn't exactly know what life she supposedly wanted back.

Matt's expression was unreadable as he buttoned his dark blue shirt. Once he was done, he sauntered up to her and put both hands on her shoulders.

"You want honesty? I miss her. I don't love who you are any less but I miss the woman I have history with. I miss the woman who trusts me, knows what I can do for her, knows my weaknesses and isn't afraid to show me hers. I miss her knowing expressions, how she can tell what I'm feeling, regardless of what I'm saying," he paused. She hoped it wasn't to give her a chance to speak because at the moment, she could barely breathe.

"I won't lie to you," he continued relentlessly. "I want my Lizzy back. I need to tell her how I feel. I remember her just the way she was, and what she means to me and I need to tell her it's safe to come home."

He leaned down to kiss her on her cheek, as if she were the stranger, he implied she was. She swallowed the lump in her throat and struggled to get the words out, "Then go get her."

CHAPTER 35

MATT

Matt cringed in the elevator of the hospital as he remembered the pained look on Liz's face before he left. He couldn't believe it when he heard it. She was terrified of getting her memory back. And he knew why. She'd lose him. Deep inside she must feel Lizzy's fear. That his wife was hiding within her. And her double was protecting her. He knew it was harsh, but it wasn't meant for her. It was meant for Lizzy. The love of his life needed to hear it. And if she didn't, then that's where the good doctor needed to come in.

Matt was ready to listen.

I should have done this weeks ago.

The elevator door opened to the neuro floor that Matt painfully remembered. If not the bright rounded dove-painted open hall that triggered the memories of that horrendous week, but the undertone scents of bleach and rubbing alcohol sure would do it. Matt paced past the busy waiting area and immediately spotted Dr. Tai, who stood by the rounded reception desk signing papers.

"Dr. Tai," Matt exhausted. "I apologize, I'm late."

The doctor barely glanced up at him. He handed the papers back to a waiting receptionist and turned to face him. "Doesn't matter, you're here. Please sign in and follow me." You would think this doctor wasn't the same man trying to reach Matt for the past few weeks.

Moments later, they were in a large private office. Matt immediately noted the bright blue floors, matching those paper-thin surgery shoe covers and caps. The rest of the room screamed hospital-white. Closed white shutters covered the windows at the back end of the room. One white, out-of-place file cabinet stood at the corner and a white table across it. There was nothing else but two white plastic chairs in the entire room. Seemed like a waste of perfectly good space in the crowded hospital.

"Please take a seat."

"Thank you," Matt nodded and sat across from the doctor. "I um, got all your voicemails."

"I assumed you would."

"I'm ready to discuss treatment plans."

"I'm happy to hear that. But I don't have a plan."

Matt was puzzled but he just glared at the doctor.

"I can't treat someone I haven't seen in nearly a month. I don't know her progress, or regression, or what state she's in," he paused. "I don't know who I'm treating," the doctor emphasized, as if to get his point across.

"She's innocent."

"What do you mean by innocent?"

"You know what I mean; she's a new person in this world, she doesn't know anything."

"No, she's not an infant; she is your wife and has lived all the things Elizabeth had lived. She just doesn't remember living it. She is no more innocent than you or I just because she doesn't remember doing something. She is, at the end of the day, the Lizzy you keep referring to."

Matt stared at him for a long moment. "She doesn't want her memory back," he finally said.

"That's fear," the doctor said without giving it so much of a thought.

"I get that. But why?"

"You tell me."

Matt jumped out of his chair, sliding it across the short end of the room. "I'm not here for a therapy session."

"Neither am I," the doctor patiently argued. "I'm here to help Elizabeth. Is she getting worse?"

"She remembers something."

"Something?"

"Yes, it wasn't exactly a memory. It was something that someone had said to her, my brother actually, and she remembered him telling her those same words."

"What were the words?"

"What does it matter?"

The doctor's expression was perplexed. "It matters tremendously!"

Matt rubbed his temples. "I don't even remember."

"Yes, you do," the doctor assured. "What's the big deal, they're just words."

And this was why Matt had been avoiding the doctor, regardless of how brilliant the magazines claimed he was. The guy was a real jerk.

"'Nothing good comes of keeping secrets'," Matt muttered. He folded his arms over his chest. "That was it."

Dr. Tai sat back in his chair and stared at Matt as though he were, in fact, in a therapy session. "Fine," the doctor briskly peeled his back off the chair and leaned forward. "Tell me what happened right before her accident."

"She was out shopping," Matt replied.

Another hard stare. "Mr. Owen, I do need you to realize that if it were an easy task bringing back an individual from lost memories, as severe as Elizabeth's case, don't you think you would have received a step-by-step in one of my voicemails? That being said, it's easy to pick out the most uneventful thing that happened that day and move on." He watched Matt for a moment before continuing. "You don't have to tell me what it is," he untwined his fingers and sat back in his chair, "but it would help."

In very few words, Matt managed to tell Dr. Tai the horrific thirty-six hours his wife had prior to her crash.

Strangely, the doctor barely seemed surprised. "Thank you. That certainly helps." After a short thought, the doctor looked up at him again. "I think I may know how to help."

Matt was ready for nearly anything. He needed her back. All of her. The woman who lied to protect what they had. The only woman he'd ever love and would always be grateful for.

"Do you think I should tell her? Make her confront herself?"

"Let's take a different approach. Telling this to Liz won't help. It might set her back, in fact. Hearing negativity about one's life usually sets them into a state of denial and fear. Start with good truths that specifically have to do with your relationship. Liz is in there somewhere. Spend time with her, focus on what she focuses on and try to remember what it might be triggering," he pushed off his chair again and leaned in. "Her mind is always being triggered, Mr. Owen, she just doesn't stop to realize it. You need to pay attention and embrace it."

CHAPTER 36

LIZ

The light knock on the door was so faint, Liz thought she might have imagined it. She hesitated for a moment before striding to the door. It couldn't have been Matt. Surely, he wouldn't be back for at least another hour. She pulled the door open and saw the last person she expected. The questionable man from the party that Matt had later insisted was nothing to worry about.

"Hello," Clyde said, his mouth curving up a bit on one side. The gesture sent chills through her.

"Hello Clyde." She sincerely hoped it sounded natural. "Matt's not home right now, so..." she half turned back to the living room as if to prove it. Something in her wanted him to leave immediately.

"That's okay," he said lightly, yet effectively pushing the door open further. "I can wait."

"I don't think that's a good idea." She turned to the man, now standing in her living room. For no known reason, her heart started thumping. The only men she'd been alone with were people she knew and trusted. Clyde... was in no uncertain terms a man to be trusted. Of that she was sure. She supposed she should feel some comfort after Matt insisted he was a friend. But not enough.

The man wasn't leaving. He plopped down on her sofa, instead. She imagined what Matt, Ben or even Megan would have said to Clyde at this moment. "Clyde, I don't have time for any childish banter today, I'll let Matt know you stopped by." She motioned out the door.

Clyde stared at her so hard she felt violated. And then mortally frightened. He relaxed his shoulders. "I know you're doubting my sincerity Lizzy, but I can assure you I'm trustworthy."

"You're right. I do doubt your sincerity." Feeling more like herself.

"Why, though? Your husband trusts me," he paused and leaned forward. "Enough to tell me what's really going on with you."

Her eyes flared.

"I know you don't remember me...or anything for that matter."

Liz hoped the shiver that shot up her spine and disbursed in her temples wasn't in any way visible.

"Matt told me," he continued when she froze.

"He told you?"

He laughed. "It's okay. I'm a friend."

She swallowed back her fury. "When?"

"Last night. I could tell something was off about you. So, he told me." He shrugged, as if it were such a simple fact.

She forced herself a quick recovery and lifted her head. "Well then you can understand why I don't feel comfortable with you here and I'd appreciate it if you left."

He stood. "Of course. I certainly don't want to make you uncomfortable. And hey for what it's worth I'm glad you and Matt were able to work things out."

She frowned on instinct. The devilish grin forming on his face told her he caught it, and she immediately regretted her slip.

He eyed her, interestingly. "Man, that must have been hard for you both. Matt especially."

She simply raised her eyebrows and looked away. Still holding the door open for him.

"And talk about timing," he pressed with exaggerated amazement. "I mean it truly is one for the books." He waited a beat then went on. "But you guys seemed to have overcome that little...well...*colossal* road bump. A power couple indeed."

"We do our best."

"No one could survive a secret like that."

She swallowed and held back so much, she didn't even know where she'd even begin. "I suppose not."

He circled around her, while she was panting silently in place. Her chest heaved. *Why was she so afraid of what he was saying?*

He leaned into her ear and whispered. "You don't know what I'm talking about, do you?"

She turned her head to face him beside her. Her eyes surely throwing daggers at the man. "Not a clue."

In a matter of sixty seconds, Clyde managed to completely destroy Liz with his words. An accusation she refused to believe. And she wouldn't have if it weren't for the undeniable tension between her husband and his brother. She wanted to scream, cry, accuse the man before her of being a liar. But all she could manage through blurred vision was to open the door and ask the wicked man to leave. She barely acknowledged the look on his face when he walked out, but she imagined that he left quite pleased.

Her chest was on fire as she made her way to the sofa. She was disoriented and the usual dull pain in her head was now blindingly sharp. It was unbearable, the pain. Which ached more, her chest or her head, she couldn't tell. She was being swallowed by short memories. Flashes of Matt being angry and seemingly resentful for no known reason. Everything was becoming clear despite her head spinning like the globe. She wondered what would possess someone to act like they loved them while being utterly disgusted. She managed to get up the stairs. There was no way she could stay in that apartment.

CHAPTER 37

MATT

It was going to be different from here on. He was going to do everything in his power to bring Liz back. He'd let it go on too long, relishing the absence of a woman who had betrayed and hurt him. Appreciated the new and innocent wife he had in her place for however long he chose. But it was wrong. He was keeping an innocent woman hostage from getting her life back. Sickened at his own actions and betrayal, he closed his eyes to pull himself together before walking back into his apartment. A deep breath helped stabilize him before entering. He knew what he would do.

He'd apologize for demoralizing her existence earlier. He couldn't understand how he thought it would help. Lizzy wouldn't hear him. She was never that easy.

Instead, he was crushing the heart of her placeholder, a woman who only had him to turn to and who opened her heart to him. He'd make it up to her. He'd make her see that it's her he loves in every way that counts, and she wasn't going away, she would just remember more of what they've shared.

The moment he walked into their apartment, the air seemed thick, and dread settled within him, his stomach locked tight as Liz emerged from the den.

Could the words he had left her with this morning have changed her? Trigger her?

She wore dark jeans and a black blouse. The colors were off for her. Since he'd brought her home from the hospital, she had seemed to prefer all of Lizzy's bright colored sun dresses.

"How was your visit with my doctor?" Her tone sent chills through him.

"Productive," he responded without looking into her eyes. "We, uh...discussed some things that might trigger your memory," he added.

"Like what?"

Matt looked up at her. "I don't know, I guess we'll know it when we come across it. I just want you to focus on the good things."

"Is that what you've been trying to do? Steer me from things I may not want to remember?" she asked curiously.

Matt narrowed his eyes at her. "Would that be a terrible thing?"

"Of course not," she started as he turned to go up the stairs. "What would be terrible is if you would keep me from remembering anything at all," her voice turned icy.

Matt turned his head back slowly to face her. A new stranger, not the innocent, curious and open-hearted woman he'd brought home weeks ago. This woman was accusing, demanding, bitter, and frigid.

"What's going on?"

"I've been trying to ask you the same thing for weeks, Matt. And you refused to give me an honest answer. You could barely look at me, blew me off with short answers to my eager questions, pretending to be preoccupied with deep concern, when you were just trying to figure out how to tell me our marriage was over," her voice grew louder and angrier.

She didn't have her memory back.

No.

This still wasn't Lizzy. This was a new side to her placeholder, as he'd recently began to refer to her. It was an easy tell. No matter how angry Liz would get, she always had a soft glow behind her eyes. Eyes that carried life, love and warmth within them.

The eyes he was looking into now were cold, hateful and hurt. The kind of hurt where you realize everything you'd been told was a lie and you really have no one to turn to. His wife would know that could never be true.

"Did my brother tell you?" he whispered after a moment.

"Was I the thing he...borrowed, Matt?" her voice breaking.

He glanced around as if there were a place he could escape her confused and hurting eyes. He swallowed, then returned her glare. "You answer my question first."

"No. Clyde did," she stated immediately.

"When?"

"It's my turn," she said through gritted teeth.

"Why was he here?" Matt shouted, his anger strong enough to overpower hers.

"You told me he was a friend, he stopped by and I let him in," she argued defensively.

Matt ran his fingers through his hair in frustration, then placed them on his hips and took a breath, an effort to control himself around her. Something he'd been struggling with a lot lately.

"When did he stop by?" he demanded, glaring at the floor.

"While you were out, but what does it matter? You're still not answering my question." She took a step toward him.

He looked at her. His expression hard. "I wouldn't put it that way. But yes...you were."

She fell back into the sofa behind her. "And you just found out?" she whispered.

The knot tightening in his stomach, he nodded, "Two days before your accident."

She held her hand to her chest. "Did I tell you?" a doubt in her voice.

He looked away. "No. You didn't."

Liz's eyes wandered for a long moment. Matt could practically see the thoughts running through her head. She stood, deeper anger shaking through her and she held her hands up, "Why did you bring me here?"

"What?"

"Why am I here? she demanded. "You walked out on me, didn't you? That's what it was. That's what I felt, wasn't it? Back at your parent's house."

He didn't answer. Instead, he swallowed some words that wouldn't help and held his gaze at the coffee table between them.

"Why did you bring me here?" she yelled, gesturing at the apartment.

"Because you needed me," he answered truthfully.

Her eyebrows shot up. "You felt sorry for me?"

"No, you're still my wife."

"You made me believe that you loved me, that we have something so amazing, why?" she cried.

Matt's temper was quickly being tested. "Because we did have something amazing."

"So, what happened? Tell me everything, I need to know."

"I'll tell you everything you *need* to know," he insisted.

"That's not exactly what I asked," her voice warry.

This wasn't going to be easy. "It's what you're going to get," he snapped. Lying to her was no longer an option. And he was surprised to find himself relieved. He couldn't bear to do any more of it.

She stilled, her dark eyes guarded and angry.

He couldn't stand seeing her so vulnerable. At that moment, he could sense how alone she felt. He wanted so much to comfort her, but it was too late for that.

"You don't need to know what happened," he softened. "That's not a part of your life you need to concern yourself with," he took a small careful step in her direction. "Yes, okay, I was angry and I continued to be after your accident, when I should have just..." his voice broke. "I should have pushed all that aside and been the man you needed, the husband you needed. Instead of...making you question my love."

Tears escaped her eyes. "Do you love me?"

"No," he crept toward her. "I don't know you. I love my wife, the woman I built memories and trust with. When we both went to Dr. Tai and he was hypnotizing you...you started to tense and cry and panic and I just—I couldn't do it that way. I couldn't let it all come crashing down on you," he stepped closer. "That's when I decided to help you myself, in my own way. No one in this world knows you better than I do, Lizzy. But then we got home and I realized—I wasn't ready. If you remembered everything, I'd have to..." he trailed off.

"End it...officially."

"No," he said abruptly and almost defensively. "I'd have to...make a decision. I wasn't ready. Especially since..."

"You were falling for the innocent stranger?"

He stared at her.

"Yeah—no one in this world knows you better than I do, either, Matt."

Raising his voice, he was inches from her. "It wasn't easy for me either Liz. I know why you lost control and crashed.

Your whole world was falling apart, but so was mine! You had it easy; you made a mistake and all you needed was a 'forgive and forget'. Well I was the one who needed to do that. I was the one who needed to find a way to live with it, to look at you and say to not only you–but to myself that it was okay," he turned and ran his fingers through his hair.

Tears rolled down her cheek and there was nothing he could say or do to stop them.

"I'm so sorry," she whispered, frozen in place.

He stepped toward her, prepared to hold her and tell her she had nothing to be sorry for. None of this was her fault. He needed her to believe her innocence. He needed her to see that he was only here to help her. To save her. He reached out to her and she pulled away, a hateful expression in her eyes.

"Don't touch me. You brought me here because you felt obligated. Because I had no place else to go,"

"Liz," he began to protest.

She ran off up the stairs.

CHAPTER 38

LIZ

Liz ran into their bedroom, frantic and angry. Her chest ached when he reached for her downstairs because she wanted him to reach her. She needed him to. But with all the strength she had left, she pulled away. She couldn't do that to him. After he'd put up with having to look at the woman who betrayed him, without confrontation, without expressing his hurt and anger. She would save him from any more of it.

She dragged out a small rolling suitcase she'd finished packing before he got home. She would give him the space he needed. Maybe one day soon, she'd wake up remembering everything and maybe Lizzy was the type of person to come crying and begging for forgiveness.

Somehow she doubted that.

There was a place she could go. You can never go wrong with family, right? The only other person in the world she had left.

"Where are you going?" Matt asked as she grabbed what she needed from the bathroom.

"I'm going to stay with Marcus," she answered as she shoved the contents of her suitcase.

"You don't want to do that," he warned. Something about the way he said it sounded haunting. As if it would be the last place she'd want to go.

"Well, I can't stay here," she replied, flatly.

"Yes, you can. You should stay here, you shouldn't be anywhere but your home."

She shut her suitcase closed, angrily. "That's what you told me weeks ago, and where did that get me? I still have no idea who I am, and I can't remember a damn thing. You've been nothing but toxic to my mind."

"Don't go to your brother's. If you wake up tomorrow and remember, you'll hate me even more than you do now, knowing I let you," he paused, anguish in his eyes. "Trust me on this," he added.

She wasn't sure why she should, but she did. But unless he gave her a reason, she wasn't going to stay. She brushed past him at the doorway, before descending the stairs. She walked past the table with the house keys and decided against grabbing them. There was only one key she needed, and she had it. She barely pulled the door open before Matt shut it.

"Liz, you can't leave. Let me help you heal, let me help you remember. You're not just leaving me, you're taking my wife with you."

"You can't keep me here," she hesitated. "Besides, I'm sure if she wanted to see you, she would have been back by now."

Matt stared at her, his expression a mixture of pain and disappointment. He slowly released the door and backed away.

*   *   *

Liz's driver pulled up on a narrow street, lined with mid-level apartment buildings. Marcus hadn't invited her, but she texted him when she left and said she was on her way over. He had sounded hesitant for a moment but then gave her the address to give the cab driver.

"Liz, I'm glad you're here. Uh, come in. He stepped aside to let her into the small apartment. Although the size of the unit didn't hit her senses as fast as the pine scent. It was an odd scent for the season, which made her scan the room further to locate its source. She had spotted it. A candle was lit on the wooden coffee table.

"Thank you." She left her bags on the hardwood floor, by the door. She b-lined for the candle and blew it out, then crossed the short distance to the double paned windows and opened one of them. Liz turned on the air conditioning that was affixed to the other. She picked up the candle, "Save this for Christmas."

He smiled and lifted her bags. "So, I started to clear out my room for you—"

"No, please leave those by the door. I'm not staying."

He frowned. "But Matt called... he said you were..."

"I know." But she didn't really know. She didn't know why she came if she weren't staying. But she needed to know why staying with Marcus was off-limits. Her only real family.

Marcus froze and approached her where she stood in the living area. "Are you okay? Matt didn't say much except to make sure you were safe."

"I had to leave."

He watched her thoughtfully, as if he'd truly missed her. A part of her was relieved to be with her brother. It wasn't just the known fact. She genuinely felt the connection. Regardless of which, it wasn't enough to ignore Matt's warning.

She sat down on his small yet comfortable black sofa. The rest of the furniture was simple, she observed, briefly scanning the room. None of which purchased with other pieces in mind. Red floor lamp by the window. A dresser that was also used as a television stand. A few open boxes scattered throughout the apartment.

"What happened?" he asked, settling next to her.

She wasn't about to go into details that he most likely didn't know and didn't really concern him. But there was something she absolutely needed to ask him.

"That's kind of what I need to know, Marc. When you came by my place...you've never been there before, have you?

"No," he admitted without hesitation.

She supposed she should have followed with 'why not?' but decided against it. She just nodded and stared at random carpet stains.

"Your decor sucks by the way," he added when she didn't say anything

She burst out laughing; it was so natural with him. "Clearly, I didn't consult with you, when I no doubt should have," she laughed again and wiped at a teary eye.

"You're welcome to stay here. For as looking as you need."

She shook her head. "Matt didn't want me coming here." She watched him, "Can you imagine that?"

He looked down. "I can Liz. You wouldn't want to be here, with me."

Fear struck her heart. And it didn't take long for her to figure out why she cared to the point where her heart would break. Had she done something awful to yet another person in her life?

"Why?" She tried to keep it together, but her throat threatened tears

He laughed nervously and stood. "I wish I knew." He threw his arms up in the air casually. Then after a short moment, he swallowed and looked at her. "I'm lying actually. I do know."

Chills ran up Liz's arms as a sudden and rapid vision passed through her.

Marcus standing across her in a large near empty house. All that surrounded them were boxes and various furniture pieces.

Somehow it reminded Liz of the storage room.

No one was saying anything. The vision was frozen, but she can feel the anger coming from her. The blazing in her chest was all too clear.

She didn't share the vision with Marcus, partly because she didn't want to interrupt his train of thought. But if she were to guess; the look on Marcus' face was what sparked the image...or dare she call it...*memory.*

His hands shook. "Our parents, Liz, were wonderful people. And they loved us to no end. More than they loved themselves. See, I always knew that. And so did you," he added quickly. "But see you never took advantage of it. After I graduated a few years ago, I moved back in with mom and dad. No biggie, right? Lots of people do that before they get a job and try to make it on their own.

It didn't sound like anything terrible to Liz.

But see, mom and dad had plans to move to Florida. It was their dream after their kids were grown up. But I stopped them from moving on with their retirement plans when I told them I was moving back in.

Liz frowned. Suddenly feeling a heaviness in her chest.

"I knew they had dreams but knowing how they'd do anything for us, I took advantage." He took a breath. "Every time you visited for the holidays, you'd berate me for it. I guess I never understood what one or two more years would be."

Liz agreed it was a little selfish of him, but not something she would hold against him forever.

He looked at her tentatively, as if he were about to say something that made it all make sense. "Less than two years after I moved back in, they went to this party..."

"The day they crashed," Liz whispered, her eyes and mind in an absolute haze.

His breath was hard and shaky. "Needless to say, your slight resentment of me, flourished into full on hatred and blame."

"That's not true." Liz cried.

"Liz?"

What the hell was that?

Those weren't the words on her tongue. Yet they were the ones that escaped. The ones that felt true to her heart. But there was anger behind them. For the life of her, she couldn't figure out why? Not in that fleeting moment where it seemed someone else was speaking for her.

Liz shook her head. "I'm sorry, I didn't mean to scream at you like that..."

Marcus either ignored her apology or didn't seem to hear it. He turned his head for a mere second as if hesitating. Then went on. "We were already rocky, you and me because of my holding them back. I mean I knew. Heck, after the initial shock, it was all I could think about."

"I don't hate you..."

"It's my fault Lizzy, you and I always knew it."

"No, you don't understand. I don't hate you. I can feel it, Marcus. Whenever you're around, I feel happy, safe, I *know* you're family. I feel most connected to you. I'm sorry about what happened to us. I can't tell you why it did, but I am sorry."

He kept his hands in his pockets. "Yeah, well there's nothing you can do, can you."

Liz frowned.

"Sorry, truth is, Liz—"

"Yes please, more truths." She was starting to regret insisting that she could handle it.

"A part of me was excited to finally see my sister, regardless of circumstances. I've missed you so much." His eyes watered and he swallowed. "I guess I'll never learn. I'll always be selfish, Liz. I was so happy to have you back in my life, I didn't want you to get your memory back," he shrugged, his hands still in his pocket. "I'll take my big sister any time, anyway, and any day." He approached her, pulled his hands out of his pocket and placed them on her shoulders. "And I'm not going to apologize for it."

CHAPTER 39

MATT

"Well can you tell me if she called another car after you dropped her off?" The cab driver on the other line was most unhelpful. "Okay. Right. Thank you." He hung up and threw the phone onto the sofa. After he'd gotten off the phone with Marcus nearly twenty minutes ago, who told him Liz wouldn't be staying with him and had no other information to offer, Matt had been frantic in his search for her. His brother-in-law showed little care in Matt's frustration, but gave him enough courtesy to call him with this very frustrating fact; *Liz took off.*

His next call was going to be his parents. But that would mean a demanded explanation of what happened. Followed by countless calls from his mother until Liz was found. He breathed out a heavy breath and ran a hand over his face, for the tenth time that hour. He needed a drink.

He sat, helpless on the couch with his whiskey on the rocks and tried to remember Liz the way she was. He was surprised at how easy it was to remember her. Her honest smiles and her 'humor you' ones. Her compassion and bravery. Her defensiveness and reason.

Reason. The thought triggered a memory for him. Once not too long ago, he sat in the den in the middle of the night, an hour after he'd walked out on Liz. Beating his brains out trying to figure out her reason. She listed quite a few that night. All of which were perfectly understandable. He took another long sip and chuckled at the vision of the man berating a woman who fought with everything she had to keep him. He shook his head and stood to pace around the living room. Something he should probably get used to since he wouldn't be getting much sleep. He needed to be honest with himself before he went after her. Besides the obvious, there was something else that was bothering him. Something else she wasn't telling him, he was sure of it.

It wasn't until his third glass, which he'd given up on adding the rocks to, did he come to recognize what that might have been. It was without a doubt the fact that it was her decision...and hers alone...to keep this from him. Sure, she'd confessed to her being the blame for keeping the secret, but it went further than that. She fully intended to take it to her grave. And possibly made Ben oblige. He'd figured it out between the brief encounters he'd had with both Ben and Megan since. Both of whom had urged her to come clean. And of course, there was Liz's memory of Ben's words.

And while on the subject of honesty, he was starting to understand the root of his anger with her secret; The fact that she lived it.

It angered him that the woman he loved had to live a lie that tortured her throughout their marriage. Not to mention, a spark that he set off. He rubbed his temples again. Lizzy would hate it if she knew he were taking the blame for her actions. And he wasn't. But it wasn't something he could ignore either.

Given the chance, he'd make it all up to her. Because, yeah, he was kidding himself before. There wouldn't be a soul in the world that would keep him from being with her.

CHAPTER 40

LIZ

"Thank you for coming for me." Liz peeled her eyes off the rainy road in the spacious and clean black SUV.

"Anything for you." Ben's expression was hard and his tone indifferent, contrary to what he'd just proclaimed.

"Just don't take me home."

"Somehow, I doubt that's where you were headed," he replied flatly.

"Thanks." Was all she was going to say. She'd leave it up to him where they'd go. She guessed to his house so she could confide in Megan. Heaven knew she wasn't about to talk to *him*. Nonetheless, it was still him she called. Something she was probably going to regret and couldn't explain. She buried her head in her hands for a second then shot him an apologetic look. "I shouldn't have called you."

Still, he refused to look at her. Which could be understood. If the wave of thunder didn't give away that you need to watch the road intensely, then the relentless waterfall over his windshield probably should. "Well, you did."

"Ben?" She hoped it came out as annoyed as she felt.

"Look, I'm sorry Liz. I'm just...sure you have questions that I'm not really prepared to answer," he barked. But the frustration seemed to be more at himself than at her. Somehow, she understood that much.

"How did you guess?"

He snickered and his expression softened. But it didn't last long. "Please tell me Matt told you."

Her chest ached again at the mention of his name. She shook her head. "I was paid a visit from Clyde."

Ben glanced at her in shock. "Son of a bitch." Ben hit the steering wheel and then immediately apologized for losing it.

"Again—not born yesterday," Liz insisted.

Ben continued to mumble under his breath. "I'm sorry, Liz. It shouldn't have happened that way." He glanced at her again, his brows narrowed. "You okay?"

She shrugged at this point. Refusing to think about it anymore. Meanwhile questions were in fact stewing in her chest, waiting to be asked, and if she didn't get them in order soon, they'd be spilling out in no particular—or coherent—order. She turned to the window to focus on the sound of the torrential rain.

"Wanna talk about it?"

"Maybe some other time," she muttered.

"That's what got you into this mess," he joked.

She laughed under her breath but kept her focus on the road. "I love him." She couldn't explain why that was all that came out.

"You have no idea how much, Liz."

"I don't want to lose him."

"I can promise you, you never will." Ben spoke almost instantly. She just glared at him. The man seemed to have an answer to everything.

"Sorry—we've had this conversation once or twice —I know my lines."

She watched him thoughtfully. "So we have."

He caught her stare and then pulled the steering wheel midway to the right, glancing behind him for a fraction of a second. It took her a moment to realize he was pulling over to the shoulder in the middle of the highway. After he'd put the car in park, he turned to her. His eyes were just as thoughtful, but held a level of certainty that she lacked.

"I'm glad you called me Liz. I've missed you. You'll probably burst out in hysterics if you happen to get your memory back mid-sentence when I say this, but don't think too far into it. You and I may have had a night together, but it was nothing—for either of us," he paused for a breath. "The truth is—I cared about you very much even then. Who you were, and what you've done for my brother. I really thought you were it for him and we may as well all fall in love with you now." he paused. "After he left...I was just as angry, and...got my emotions mixed up." He reached for her hand. "We're close...but we're in no way romantically connected." He pulled back, a playful smirk on his face. He pulled up his collar dramatically. "Sorry to disappoint you, kid."

She did laugh, as he'd predicted. "Thank you for setting me straight, Romeo." She laughed again and wiped away a tear, as Ben put the car back in drive and eased back into traffic.

Less than an hour later, Ben pulled up to his garage. Unlike her and Matt, Ben and Megan lived in a small house by the beach, closer to where the Owen's lived, Matt's parents. The rain finally slowed to a drizzle and it started to approach the early evening. She was grateful for Meg not being much of a talker. After she made Liz some tea, she sat with her in the kitchen and just listened. Megan was good at that. And she wasn't fooling anyone. Behind her cold exterior, there was a woman who did care for her family— and cared for Liz as a friend.

"I don't know whether you're the confidant type, but you're all I have."

Megan shrugged and her lips curved. "You're kind of all I have too." She pulled on a white bakery box on the kitchen island. "And don't worry about Matt," she started to say with a mouth full of cannoli, "he'll be keeping his distance for a few days."

Liz frowned.

"He called while Ben was picking you up, wondering if we'd heard from you." She stopped to watch Liz. "I told him you'd be safe here with us."

I was safe with him too.

"Thank you." Liz fell into an absent daze, thinking about Matt for longer than she'd planned to let herself. Then she noticed something about Megan's lavender sweater.

"Hey, when are you going to give me back that sweater?"

Megan jerked her head back and lowered her chin, "This sweater?"

"Of course, that sweater, you didn't think I'd recognize it? You borrowed it last summer because Ben is always blasting the AC in here. And you said—"

"This is the perfect summer color..." they both said in unison. Only Megan's words were more mumbled.

"Liz...you remember that?"

Liz considered the odd question for only a fraction of a second. Until it wasn't odd anymore.

And she couldn't answer it.

She could barely find coherent words much less figure out how she'd remembered the menial fact. She continued to stare at her sister-in-law, hoping for something else, anything else, regardless of its significance.

But nothing came. She breathed out. It was so fast. So small. And so unfair.

She shook her head and turned away. Thankfully, Megan didn't pressure her and just stood after a moment and made more tea.

Throughout the night, Liz experienced other small memories, but kept those to herself. It was as if her brain was mocking her with these tiny visuals. Very few of which contained an audible memory. She barely heard much of what Ben and Megan rambled about after they sat up drinking wine and picking at more baked goods. If she hadn't known any better, she'd say the couple was afraid to let her go to sleep. The two sat on the couch across from the one she sat on. Their spacious living area and open kitchen only held two white sofas, an oak coffee table, and a sixty-plus inch television over a wood-burning fireplace. There was very little carpet, which was intentional, no doubt, to avoid covering the glossy, dark wood floors.

"I'm going to be okay, guys. And to be honest, I barely heard anything you said for the past hour." Liz gave a lazy smile through her sleepy voice.

Ben looked at Megan tentatively then back at Liz. "We know. And I think I know at what points you had other memories too, Lizzy."

Megan smiled. "Ben's pretty good at picking up on when people have tuned him out." She shrugged and winked at her husband.

"Honestly, Liz," Ben continued, "we don't know how fast these are coming back and if you happen to wake up... confused...we want to be here for you."

Liz laughed. "So what, you guys are going to take turns being watch guards? Thank you, but I don't need it." She laughed again to conceal how utterly alone she felt at that moment. But not scared. Remembering who she was didn't scare her. She was eager for it, in fact. More ready for it than she'd ever been.

But she knew better than to stress or rush the memories or to ask questions. The only time she would remember something is when she wasn't searching or questioning or feeling much. The visions faded into her mind and just as simply, faded out. Not all had meaning.

But the loneliness. That was real. And the first time she'd felt it in weeks. Seeing Ben and Megan standing over her, working together in their secret way of communication. It was so solid. So honest. As if everything they did—they did together. How wholesome it must feel for them.

That was what she needed the most. She breathed in deep, forcing the pain away from her chest. She needed to fight these emotions that kept her prisoner. It was the only way to get better.

On her own.

The next morning Megan proposed to move Liz into a fully furnished rental her firm had recently listed. Thanks to Megan's strong relationship with the developer, they allowed Megan's "immediate family" to rent the unit for a minimum of one month before they put it back on the market.

Liz knew she couldn't avoid Matt that long. But at a minimum, a few days was more than necessary for both of them.

The offer didn't come from nowhere. Liz had thanked them for the stay for the night but insisted that she probably should go back to her brothers, or get a hotel for a few days. The idea of having her disappear must have crossed their mind because Megan immediately offered the vacant townhouse, until she was ready to go home.

Two days into her new living arrangement, Liz was starting to control her memories. Recalling those she focused on. But it didn't come easy. She picked up a pattern in her state of mind when memories would come. She needed to be calm, patient and by no means hasty or stressed. Her mind's demands were not easy to meet.

Liz and Marcus had taken a trip back to the storage unit to bring some things back to Liz's temporary home. He wanted to help shuffle through. But Liz insisted on giving fate a chance, and grabbed a few random boxes, and two small furniture pieces.

"I just wanted to make this place my own for as long as I'm here, you know?" She told him when they were back at her place later that night. So far, they'd only gone through one box together and placed the one lamp she grabbed at the last minute on the side table by the pale blue sofa. She set her tea down on the oversized marble coffee table and sat back, exhausted.

"Well it's a good thing we kept them all, then."

Liz caught a flash of hesitation after Marcus spoke the words, as if he weren't sure about them. She was about to question why they wouldn't, when a harsh memory invaded her otherwise peaceful mind frame.

Her and Marcus are in their parent's house. The same vision she had just a few days ago when she was with him. Only this time, she heard everything. Liz stood surrounded by boxes and various pieces of furniture. Many of them more vivid in this vision. She had been crying. Her throat ached and she was screaming at Marcus. Hurtful words, accusations being thrown between the two of them. No. Not between the two of them. Just Liz at her brother.

It was painful to relive, but not a shock, thankfully. Since Marcus was honest to a fault with her.

She pulled herself out this time. The raw memory didn't fade like all the others. She looked up at her little brother. Her eyes burned. *She loved him.* She loved him insanely. She loved him enough to pounce on him and tackle him to the bare floor.

The way she used to when they were kids.

But along with that love that she remembered clearer than day, came an unfair crushing reality of how she'd left him nearly two years ago.

She stood and burst into an uncontrollable cry. She looked at Marcus, whose face was now covered with concern. She opened her mouth—an apology she desperately needed to get out caught in her throat. "Marcus..." she choked, and before she could even attempt another word, he crossed to her and pulled her in. Her brother's warm embrace was the painkiller she desperately needed that moment. She closed her eyes. She wasn't sure how long he'd held her, but it was enough to get her breathing normally again.

"Oh, that's definitely my sister's hug." He grasped her shoulders and stepped back, studying her. A warm smile formed on his blurry face. She quickly rubbed her eyes to look at him once more. Then threw herself at him again.

"I'm so sorry, Marc."

"Oh, come on Lizzy, you know I never take you seriously," he joked. He was good at that. And though she could argue that he never did in fact take her seriously, she knew he'd been hurt. "Don't worry about me—about us. You need to take a minute. Sit, I'll make you something." He guided her back to the paper-rough sofa.

She wiped at her tears and sat back down, staring into space for probably longer than any normal human could possibly handle. Marc had returned with a plate of food for her and a glass of water. She hadn't even heard him bustling in the open kitchen. It was her entire childhood and young adult life that was now all clear. If she sat here and tried, she could recall every memory up until Matt.

All memories of him were still hazy. She absently admired the lamp placed by the sofa. She ran a finger over the tarnished golden tube, remembering its shine from when it lived in her father's den. She smiled at it until she noticed a small crack on the edge of the glass shade. She reached for it and another memory struck her.

"*Gone, I want it all gone. I don't want any of it.*"

"*Liz, you're just angry—you don't even know what some of this stuff is...*" *Marcus tried to argue with her.*

"*I said throw it out,*" *she barked. She hadn't noticed it before, but Matt was there too. He'd been standing by the entrance, holding some oversized trash bags and talking with a truck driver who had come to pick up certain furniture pieces for donation. She remembered his eyes when he watched her in her frenzy, tossing random objects into trash bags and boxes. And the lamp, she tossed it with too much force, knowing she could break the fragile thing. But she also remembered her pausing to see the damage she caused, and the rest of the memory faded out.*

She turned to her brother, seeing him in a new light. "Marc, you went back for all the stuff? I watched them drive away with everything." Liz was impressively shocked. Not that her brother would do something so sentimental, but the fact that he'd been so careful and organized about it. He somehow managed to let her think everything was gone. Rented an enormous storage unit and managed to keep up its monthly payments. That in itself was the biggest shocker.

Marcus chuckled uncomfortably and shrugged. "I wish I could take the credit. But that was all Matt."

"Matt?" her pleased expression faded and was replaced with a spark somewhere between her stomach and chest.

"Yeah, he...well he was there that day—with us at mom and dad's—when you insisted every last item in that house get tossed." He raised his eyebrows as if to point out her nonsense. "And I didn't know this at the time, but apparently he paid the guys from the church to take the boxed items and a few of the furniture pieces to a storage unit." He held his hands up, "Not everything though. A lot of their furniture did in fact need to go." Marcus glanced at the unopened boxes by the entrance. "Anyway, he'd given me an extra key and told me to keep it between us for a while." Her brother shrugged.

She nodded slowly. "He knew I'd regret it eventually. That I'd miss them and want to shuffle through these things again."

"I know it's painful Lizzy." He handed her the plate of food. "But you don't have to go through it alone."

She popped a cube of cheese and grinned at him. "So, you'll stay with me tonight?"

CHAPTER 41

MATT

It had been nine days since she left. Knowing Liz was safe and Megan was checking in on her daily, was the only thing that kept him from running to her. Marcus had texted him too—all of twice—to let him know about Liz's slow but sure recovery. Finally, he decided enough was enough.

Matt walked a few houses down and glanced once again at Megan's text; fifty-six. The cookie cutter townhouses were painted blue and white. They all had the same concrete steps that pulled up to a single large door. Matt finally reached the house number that matched the one on his screen. His chest tightened. He took a breath, lifted the round bronze latch, and knocked. With his heart pounding, he waited. Not knowing what her reaction would be. If she would remember him. All of him. Every part of who they are. Were. Would she still be angry at him for lying to her? With or without her memories? He wondered if he should turn around, give her more time. It comforted him to know she was safe. But it also didn't. She still wasn't with him.

He knocked again.

Nothing.

He let out another breath, disappointed and dropped his head. He stared at the blue doormat for a moment.

He frowned and stepped off it, then bent down to lift the heavy mat. A few inches in, he spotted it; a shiny silver key.

He reached for it and stood, smiling to himself and shaking his head. He slipped the key in and turned the knob, letting himself in.

Lavender and vanilla scents filled his nostrils. The apartment was furnished in pale blues, sea greens and off whites. But there were a few artifacts that looked out of place. And familiar. Matt stepped further in. The place was quiet.

"Liz?"

But he knew the place was empty. She'd gone out.

Where would she go? He could call her, but what would he say?

The house was relatively close, and similar to Ben and Megan's, so he knew the back door would lead straight to the beach. Stepping out the back door, he followed a narrow fenced in walkway and made his way down the short steps to the beach. His eyes searched for her familiar figure. It was barely ten in the morning. The sun was strong, but not unbearably hot. Lawn chairs and umbrellas were starting to unfold.

Matt strolled past the busy boardwalk. Past the gift shops, restaurants, and ice cream carts. The crowd that typically piles up around lunchtime, was starting earlier that Saturday. Liz loved strolling past the boardwalk, so that's what he would do. She could have been in the complete opposite direction, for all he knew, but he'd look for her until he found her.

Somewhere past the busier part of the beach, the boardwalk ended and an unflattering and untamed field started. Matt jumped down to the patchy grass area surrounding the land. He crossed a deserted narrow bike lane and spotted a peaceful, serene pier further along the beach. He could see past the fence and didn't see a single soul. He stopped and let out another disappointment breath. He was sure this was where Liz would have gone.

Before he turned around, he spotted an opening in the fence, also surrounded by bushes and small trees. It was elevated, so there had to be steps going down to the beach. But that wasn't what caught his attention. It was the fabric of a pale colored dress that stood out. He neared and something dropped to his stomach. At the same time, relief washed through him as he saw the back of his wife's seated body. Everything surrounding her was now hazy and it was as if he couldn't get to her fast enough. He paused, aware that his shadow might frighten her, and opened his mouth to call to her but she turned at the sound of his footsteps.

A mix of surprise and fear in her eyes. She also appeared as if she wanted to say something. Maybe his name? Or ask why he was here. But instead, she smiled with relief. It may also have been the sheer exhaustion he knew she was feeling. Her limbs looked weak and her eyes dark and drained. She was still beautiful, and he wanted more than anything to tell her that. But there was something else in her eyes. He noticed it immediately.

They were familiar and gazed up at him in a familiar way. It was Lizzy. He was sure of it. He remembered Megan's hopeful words. *She's been in and out.*

"Okay if I sit?"

She nodded and looked down at the empty space next to her. He sat beside her, inches away.

Her eyes narrowed. "How did you find me here?"

"Did you doubt that I could?"

She turned to the horizon and watched it intently. She was visibly nervous by his presence, and it shouldn't have been that way.

"Lizzy?" He knew his voice sounded hopeful and prayed that he wouldn't be hurting her if it wasn't.

She nodded and batted her eyes in the playful way he always knew. "It's me."

Unable to hold back anymore, he reached out a hand and gently placed it on the side of her face.

He searched her eyes as if it weren't enough that she'd merely confirmed it was her. All of her.

LIZ

The sun may have been hiding behind the clouds, but the warmth of his palms spread through her. Giving her the hope that she'd been silently yearning for. Though she realistically hadn't seen him in just over a week, she'd felt as though it was an eternity. She wanted to cry, to bury herself in his chest. Tell him how much she'd missed him. But the part she couldn't explain was the desire to bury herself under the warm sand at that very moment to avoid looking into his eyes.

When he showed no sign of letting her off the hook, she found the courage and lifted her head. Pure shock hit her as unmistakable remorse was all over his face. He brushed his fingers over the healing wound on her head.

"Matt."

"Baby. You're back," he smiled brightly, and a sheen of liquid filled his eyes and the hope inside her swelled.

"I heard you missed me."

She watched him ponder that for a moment before he smiled. "Yes, as much as I was grateful you were still alive, your memories and your love are everything to me and I couldn't wait to have them back."

His words left her breathless for merely a second before a sigh of relief and a few tears escaped her.

"Why didn't you come back when you remembered?" he whispered.

She looked up at him and raised an eyebrow. "Because I remembered." Her voice was hoarse. Before she could try and pull away, he pulled her into his hard torso and held her close. He squeezed a hand full of her hair, then ran his fingers along the strands. She never wanted him to let go.

"Where did you go?" He pulled back and searched her eyes.

"I feel like I've been waking up slowly. At first it was scary because I was falling in and out of myself and I was so confused. But Marcus has been helping me stay on track."

"I wish I knew. I wish I was there."

"Apparently, you need to know all the screwed-up facts about your life in order to bring you back to it." Liz laughed bitterly.

"I don't think that's entirely true."

"Well it was in my case." She said, wiping away one of her last tears.

His eyes were starting to play tricks on her; turning dark and glossy as he stared at her. Unreadable. He blinked and swallowed. "I let you down. You needed to trust someone and I..."

"You protected me. You cared for me. You put aside all your anger to try and prove to me how much you loved me." She wouldn't let him take any blame and waited until he looked at her again. "Thank you. I didn't deserve that."

"Liz, we don't need to talk about that right now," he said softly.

"What's the point of putting it off?" She shrugged. "I'm tired, Matt. Yes, to answer your question, it was very difficult keeping it from you. Painful in fact." She swallowed and blinked at the wind. "And I know this is going to sound selfish...but the dread that I felt every time I even pondered the idea..." she shook her head uncontrollably and he immediately grasped her head in his hands again. The understanding in his eyes were so clear, as though he felt her pain. She pushed his arms down and stepped back a few feet. "You were right to assume...to doubt me weeks ago," she sighed heavily. "When I told you that I made the decision to keep this from you, there was something I was leaving out." Liz glanced up to see him watch her patiently with his head cocked to the side.

"Does this have to do with my brother trying to convince you to tell me?"

She nodded slowly. "He was going to tell you regardless," she started, to test how much he knew. By the puzzled expression on her husband's face, she concluded not as much.

"I don't understand, why didn't he?"

"A few days before our wedding, he told me he had to." she continued, relieved more than she was scared. "I told him to go for it...and then wait to see if I still walk down that aisle...knowing that I'm marrying someone who will *never* look at me the same way." She let out a shaky breath, the emotions of that night flooding back. She laughed bitterly. "He was so convinced that you would understand and that I was being foolish," she shrugged as if to say the rest is history. She had since then apologized profusely to Ben for her threat on breaking it off with Matt, regardless of his forgiveness. Being the incredible friend Ben still was, he apologized for "interfering" and insisted it was her call, but gave her that very warning Liz remembered back at the hospital.

She had indeed turned her one mistake into many unforgivable ones. She wanted to sink into the sand right where she stood. It was over and she was beyond exhausted.

Matt gazed at her, his brows were creased and his mouth slightly open. Everything about his expression completely unreadable. A short moment passed before he spoke. "Did you mean it?"

She shook her head. "I don't think so." Her voice was hoarse. "I've replayed those words in my head a thousand times, and no matter how much I wanted to believe them...I don't think they were true." She watched him push some sand around with his shoe, his hands in his pockets. His avoidance now making her anxious. She was pretty certain this wasn't what the doctor had in mind when he told her to take it easy for a few weeks. She took a few more steps back to lean against the concrete wall beside the steps. Giving him the time he clearly needed.

Not a beat passed before he sauntered the few short steps to reach her, pressing her further into the cool rocky wall. He stood over her, making her lift her head to look at him. "There's something I've been meaning to tell you too." His voice was low but then a smile played on his lips. "My love for you isn't conditional. It never was and won't ever be."

She dropped her head. He had a way with words. But she hoped for more.

He lifted her chin. "Lizzy, if there was the slightest chance that it would have compromised what we had back then..." he smiled brighter. "then I am undoubtedly forever grateful, that you never spoke a word of it."

She let out an audible breath she hadn't realized she was holding. She let him embrace her once more. The need he had to protect her from her pain was profound.

"But it wasn't just about us," she said after a long moment.

Matt sighed. "Yes, yes I know. My brother." He swallowed and the resentment flashed back in his eyes. "I'll do it for you Liz. But I can't promise it will be soon."

She nodded, relieved. She may not have been proud of it, but part of her threat was to protect Matt's relationship with his brother. She opened her mouth to say as much, but he immediately put his fingers over it. "No. We're not spending any more time on this. I've been away from you long enough, and you have some nerve making me work for it. Now I'm going to kiss you and then you're going to say you're sorry for all the heartache you'd caused me the last few weeks. Yes, I am fully putting the blame on you, miss *I need some time off...*"

But she beat him to it. Shutting him and his banter off before he said something that would make him rethink kissing her at all.

He kissed her back, and she loved the force behind his smiling lips while lowering his hands to her waist. The kiss seemed to last forever. Neither one willing to let go. How this kiss did not bring back years of memories for her before, she'd never understand. But she would never forget it now. And, something told her, neither would he.

EPILOGUE

ONE MONTH LATER

MATT

The grey clouds completely dominated the sky that early Friday morning, keeping the sun from shining its rays on Liz's face. He dragged her out for what had become their ritual since they'd moved into the beach house a few weeks ago. Watching the sunrise followed by morning coffee and walks along the shore before the crowd hit. It was still warm but not warm enough for Lizzie. She was bundled in her oversized shawl. Perhaps a cloudy morning wasn't ideal to be up so early, but it was the last weekday he had with her before she went back to work, and he wanted to make the most of it.

Liz looked up at him with skepticism in her eyes yet somehow looked completely at peace. "Why are we out here, again?"

He looked out toward the horizon, as if willing the skies to clear. "Because it's basically our last day of summer. School is starting next week and you'll be back to jetting out at the crack of dawn."

She narrowed her eyes accusingly. "So you figured it would be a terrible idea to let me sleep in today."

He shot her a guilty grin, but knew she loved their early mornings at the beach; rain or shine. Although the rain was usually unexpected yet twice as enjoyable.

He couldn't believe how blind he'd been to her desire to

live by the shore. Until he found her there that day, sitting on the same steps they now sat, staring out into the horizon that had proven to be her haven. It was incredible what the ocean waves did for her. Including flooding her back with all her memories. The memories that finally brought his Lizzie back to him.

The morning serenity was also where she found the peace she needed to forgive herself. Matt liked to think he may have helped a little with that. He walked with her as she opened up about her past fears and regrets and all the moments she had ached with guilt. Her longing to a happily ever after in an honest marriage. His heart broke for her, but at the same time relieved for the end of her suffering.

He never once let her reveal anything to him without holding her hand. He had spent every day this past month proving that she was his happily ever after just as much as he was hers.

He stood, pulling her up from the cool concrete and wrapped the shawl tightly around her. She turned in his arms to rest her head against his chest.

"Thank you," she said quietly after the sound of the tide washed away.

"For?"

"For being everything I needed these past few weeks."

He wanted to tell her that it didn't compare to what she had gone through to protect what they had. Another thing he tried to convince her of the past month. She wasn't a liar. She never betrayed him. She made a mistake and didn't know how to deal with it. Instead he kissed the top of her head and breathed her in. Silently letting her know he would always be there for her.

She shivered and turned to snuggle into him. Putting

complete dead weight against his body. "You know, except for letting me sleep," she murmured into his shirt.

His lips curved on one side. "Don't worry, I'll make sure you get plenty of rest when the time comes."

She rolled her eyes. She knew him better than to say things like that without meaning. "Ah, the baby talk again."

"I told you, we can wait as long as you want. I for one, love having you all to myself. But I also can't wait to start a family with you...and of course practicing...practicing is fun."

She looked up at him lazily and hummed. "That. That is what we should be doing." She slipped her arms off him and started up the steps.

He grabbed her hand and spun her back, pulling her against his hard chest and kissed her furiously. The excitement in her to practice making a baby threw him over the edge. He pulled away, wiping her mouth. "Not this morning," he said regrettably.

She sighed. "The closing."

"The closing on our new beach-house. And then..." he let his eyes wander from side to side, "yep, no, I think that's pretty much it."

Liz punched him playfully. "And then you and Ben are going to help your dad with Sydney."

He blew out a breath in defeat. He and his brother weren't nearly back to where they used to be. But he no longer hated the guy. A few days after Matt moved into the beach house that Liz occupied during her recovery, she called Ben over. She needed to apologize for making him keep their secret...in ways she wasn't entirely proud of. He left the two alone. But not for Ben. For Liz. His only aim those days was to prove he trusted her. Also, the better half of him knew it was for the best they had that conversation in private.

"Right. Sydney," he muttered. He had almost forgotten about the promise that they'd both made their father about going with him to donate the boat.

"I'm never going to stop trying to make things right between you two," Liz said grimly.

He nodded and started up the path with her. "Well then you really will need your powernap."

When they reached the house, they found Ben at their door with his truck parked in their driveway. Considering he and Megan only lived a few blocks down the same street, they weren't completely caught off guard.

Liz waved hello and kissed Matt before going inside, no doubt back in bed.

Matt looked at his watch. "Hate to break this to you, but we have a closing in an hour. We're not doing the Sydney thing until later."

"As soon as you sign those papers, we need to get to the other side of the beach to Mom and Dad's. I got some parts," Ben announced proudly.

Matt's brows shot together, as he stalked over to the truck. "What did you do?"

"It's more about what I can't do, Matt. I can't go over there today and tell Dad it's time to donate Sydney so they could rip 'er for parts," he took a breath. "I made a list of everything she needs." His hands shook as he handed his brother a folded piece of paper.

Matt looked at the list of everything that has been causing Sydney's ultimate downfall. He peeked into the back of the truck. "Ben this must have cost a fortune."

"Do you remember the last time Mom and Dad were happy?"

Matt nodded, still focusing on the splayed mechanical parts. "When they're sailing."

"Which they haven't done in years."

Matt knew being back on the boat wasn't going to solve their parent's recent problems. But it was a damn good start. He tapped a hand against the back of the truck. "Alright, but I'm splitting this with you."

"Nah, you practically paid for it with Megan's commission on your new house."

Matt chuckled and shook his head, starting for his front door. "Ten o'clock," he called back to his brother.

"See you then."

Liz watched Matt from the kitchen with a fresh cup of coffee in her hands. "Change of plans?"

"You heard?"

"I just opened the window for air," she shrugged.

"What do you think?"

She lifted an eyebrow. "I think you make a great team."

He took his shoes off, drew the drapes together over their front windows and met her in the kitchen. She watched him with a slow smile tugging at her lips as he neared. She knew the look he was giving her, and made a good decision setting her coffee down. "We do have one hour..." He put his hands on her waist. "Would be a waste spending it drinking coffee." Effortlessly, he lifted her up on the counter and grazed the inside of her thighs.

She shivered at his touch and began to giggle. "Think we'll make it upstairs?"

He grabbed the back of her knees and slid her against him. "Not a chance." He slipped his fingers into her hair and silenced her amusement with his lips. He pulled back seconds later to look into her eyes again, savoring the joy in them. "I love you. More than you can ever imagine."

Her eyes glossed but she held back and simply nudged him. "You don't give me enough credit." Then pulled him back onto her lips.

ACKNOWLEDGEMENTS

Thank you to my readers. I hope you all enjoyed Matt and Lizzie's story. Their story was as much a rollercoaster for me to write as it was for you to read.

Thank you to my wonderful ARC Team (advance review copy) I just decided I shall call you Roxanne's Rocks! I could not have picked a better bunch. Your feedback was everything!

To Amala – for creating a show-stopping cover! Your work and vision on this couple was incredible and your guidance throughout is something I will never forget.

To Shana – my brilliant editor, for polishing my writing and helping me keep the pace. This thing would have been a mess without you.

To Stephanie – for proofreading round two; but mostly for your love and support. You remind me every day what true friendship is.

To David – for being my number one fan and supporter… and also for putting up with my thinking out loud…and basically being my walking thesaurus.

ABOUT THE AUTHOR

Roxanne's Tully grew up in New York City, where she studied theatre and stage management. Her passion for writing and storytelling started very young and every story had to have its beginning, middle and end – even if it never made it on paper.

While her genre was never limited, she now enjoys writing contemporary romance, creating realistic heroines with relatable rising actions.

A traditionalist at heart, Roxanne loves spending time in bookstores, diving into exciting new titles. She now lives in New Jersey with her real-life male hero and two children.

Lightning Source UK Ltd.
Milton Keynes UK
UKHW042200150223
417096UK00007B/64